DEMON KEPT

A RESURRECTION CHRONICLES NOVELLA

M.J. HAAG

Shattered Glass
—— PUBLISHING ——

ISBN 978-1-63869-016-0 (eBook Edition)
ISBN 978-1-63869-017-7 (Paperback Edition)

Proofreading by The Proof Posse
Cover design by Shattered Glass Publishing LLC
© Depositphotos.com

To my fey readers,
Thanks for being daring with me!

Sometimes the past won't die

Shelby has suffered at the hands of her husband for too long. Rather than endure another beating, she risks everything and escapes with the creatures who brought about the downfall of the world.

The fey aren't as horrible as her husband made them out to be. Sure they can kill with a flick of their fingers, but they're also loyal, built like gods, and craving female affection. With the fey, Shelby might finally find a sense of safety and even a second chance at learning what real love looks like.

But it'll take more than one fey to keep her safe from a past that isn't yet ready to be history.

CHAPTER ONE

You are hereby exiled from Tenacity.

The words wouldn't stop repeating in my head as we left behind the only protection we had from the infected and hellhounds. I had no more tears to cry over what had happened, but that didn't make leaving any easier.

"Move, Shelby," Nat, my husband, said with a nudge to my back. "And walk quietly. You bring any infected down on us and we'll leave you."

I glanced at him, taking in his short blonde hair and bruised cheek, and knew Nat's empty threats for what they were. He wouldn't leave me behind. Ever. If I had thought for a moment he would, I would have begged Matt, the leader of Tenacity, to let me stay. But I knew Nat and I were a package deal. End of story. I belonged to him because I'd stupidly said, "I do," a few months before the world split open and everything went to hell. Two little words had fucked over my life, and I knew he wouldn't release me from that promise. Not ever.

Nat moved ahead of me, leading the way around Tenacity's massive wall of recycled metal vehicles. I didn't know where we were headed and didn't really care. It wouldn't be as safe as the place we were leaving.

You are hereby exiled from Tenacity.

Thirteen of us, kicked out for stealing food and worse. Resentment and shame ate at me for my part in all of it.

As the sun rose higher, we parted ways with Tenacity's expansive wall and moved deeper into the surrounding trees. The hush in the woods increased my tension as I watched for any sign of movement. I walked softly, aware of each dry crunch under my feet where snow mixed with leaves and twigs.

This wasn't my first time outside the wall. But it was my first time without the hulking presence of the fey. Without one nearby, our group didn't stand a chance against the infected.

Nat interrupted that depressing line of thinking by stopping next to a thick tree. His gaze swept the group, and he waved one of his guys forward. The man scurried up the hacked off branches and pulled a wrapped bag from the crook of the tree. He silently tossed it down to Nat, who opened it and started handing out weapons. Wicked knives, a few hatchets, and a handgun, which he tucked into the back of his pants.

I could see Nat's self-righteous smirk. He thought he was so smart to have a hidden cache of weapons. But had he simply worked with the people in Tenacity, he wouldn't have needed to prepare for exile. We could have remained safely hidden behind a secure wall instead of walking God-knew-where. What good would a few knives be tonight when hellhounds howled in the distance? None. And deep down, he knew it too, but he would never openly admit it. Which was why the group made several more stops to collect more weapons and a pack filled with food.

Each stop...each supply added to the subtle undercurrent of noise from our passage. The soft clank of metal cans shifting. The rasp of bramble against packs. The crunch of sound under our feet. It carried through the trees, and eventually, I heard a distant groan.

We didn't stop moving. The plastic grip of my knife's handle bit into my palm as I clutched it and kept pace with the group.

The first infected came running at us from between the trees. While I'd left Tenacity a few times for supplies and had seen my fair share of infected, it never got easier to witness the fate of those bitten. Zombie wasn't a term I'd thought I would ever use. But the woman running toward us was just that. An undead human, decaying, yet moving.

Two men from our group worked together to bring her down. Three more infected appeared and died just as quickly. The efficiency with which Nat and his group worked surprised me. They typically went out for wood and came back in with very little. I realized now they hadn't spent their time chopping firewood. They'd been preparing. Practicing. Making an "escape" plan as if Tenacity had been such a horrible place to live.

We picked up speed, almost jogging, before we emerged from the trees onto a parking lot. Nat didn't pause. He crossed the distance to an apartment complex and grabbed a rope hanging down from a third story corner balcony.

"Billy, get up there, and get that ladder down."

The man grabbed the rope and climbed it quickly. Seconds later, a bundle of knotted rope and wooden slats dropped from above.

"Shelby, go," Nat said.

I hurried up the ladder, my limbs shaking hard. Filled in with cinder blocks, the second-story balcony no longer existed. Above that, boards extended from the floor of the next balcony. The ladder hung between a gap in the platform's planks.

As soon as I reached the top, Billy helped me over the black iron railing, and I moved back to allow the next person up while I looked around.

Three small tents dominated the space. A composting toilet sat out in the open, and a rain barrel set up near the railing. Bricks covered the sliding doors to the apartment, and a large metal storage locker sat in front of the new wall.

"Welcome home, Shelby," Nat said, joining me. "Thanks to our foresight, we have food, water, shelter, and a pretty nice setup to avoid infected and hellhounds." He wrapped an arm around me and pulled me close to kiss my temple. "You'll be living like a queen here."

I highly doubted that, but was smart enough to keep my skepticism from my face and tone.

"Thank you, Nat. I know you worked hard to make this a possibility."

"That's right. I did." He pulled back and turned me so he could study my expression. "And you're grateful for that, right?"

The infected terrified me. But my husband scared me more.

"I am very grateful," I murmured, going to my toes to kiss his lips lightly.

He grunted, apparently satisfied, and moved away to talk to the other men. I went to the railing and looked down from my prison. The ladder was up, and boards extended in its place, making climbing up to the balcony impossible.

Below us, the parking lot lay empty of infected.

"Pretty sweet setup, right?" one of the men said, coming to stand beside me. "Nat was smart to have us work on this instead of cutting wood for a bunch of freeloaders."

I said nothing but internally laughed at his entitled blindness. They were supposed to have been cutting wood for all the people in Tenacity while other people had been out gathering other supplies. Pitching in and working together. But Nat had gotten it into his head that the workload had been unevenly distributed. That some people were taking more risks than others and were "owed" more because of it.

"Look at what we have here," the guy next to me said under his breath before straightening away from me. "One of those grey bastards followed us."

Nat stopped conferring with another man to come stand beside us.

"The oak tree near the corner of the lot," the man said. "See him?"

I did. The fey casually leaned against the tree, studying us as we studied him. He was close enough and large enough that I could see the extended line of his pointed ears, and his long hair hung to his shoulders and sported multiple braids. The grey cast of his skin almost blended with the tree. If not for his light tan leather pants, which all his kind tended to favor, he would have been harder to spot. Maybe.

His size alone made him sort of hard to miss. That and the way his biceps bulged when he crossed his arms. The material of the human shirt he wore stretched to capacity to accommodate him.

He was a beast. A deadly, well-muscled beast made to fight the infected and hellhounds. And I recognized this one from the night before. He'd been one of the fey in the house with

June, the woman Nat and his men had meant to rob. He'd knocked out the men with almost no effort and then tied them up. They hadn't stood a chance against him.

"What do you think he's doing?" the man asked when Nat said nothing.

Nat quietly considered the fey for another long moment.

"Waiting to see what we do," he said finally. "I'm guessing he wants to make sure Shelby here is safe. This could work to our advantage."

A shiver of worry stole through me.

"Which tent is ours?" I asked. "I think I want to lie down for a bit."

"The orange one. But make us lunch first, Shell. You and I can have a little nap and cuddle after."

CHAPTER TWO

I took my sweet-ass time making lunch while listening to Nat spout his bullshit about how we were going to survive on the cramped balcony. Delusional and mean. Why couldn't people come with name tags that described their personalities? I would have known to steer clear of him then.

"Shelby, are you almost done or what? We're starving here."

"It's done." I turned off the camp stove and moved away from the side table. The guys converged on the food.

Keeping a pleasant smile on my face, I returned to the railing. I knew better than to take anything for myself until they finished.

Nat came over to me.

"I'm not sure I like your attitude today, Shell. You're coming across as a little high and mighty. Do you think you're special because the fey didn't knock you around last night?"

My stomach clenched. Nat was always happy to show me I wasn't better than him.

"Never. What they did to you was wrong, Nat. The fey had no right to be in Tenacity."

He nodded slowly, scrutinizing me. "They didn't. Yet, they were. And they knocked me out cold. How did that make you feel?" He reached up and smoothed back a piece of my hair, his fingers drifting down my throat. I felt sick with the need to get away. To hide.

"Terrified. I'd never been more afraid in my life," I said with complete honesty. The reason behind my fear had little to do with the fey, though, and everything to do with the man before me. Nat loved retribution. It didn't matter if it was for a perceived offense or something that actually happened.

"Your place is with me," he murmured. "Always."

"Always," I echoed, hating the finality of it. There would never be an escape for me—only a lifetime of suffering.

He let his hand drop to his side and kissed my cheek.

"Go eat. I'm ready to have some alone time with you."

A tingle hit me in the sinuses, and I ducked my head as I hurried away. Crying would only make things worse, and I didn't want worse. I wanted better and needed to figure out how to make that happen.

Behind me, the men started talking while they ate.

"We should charge him a can of food if he wants to stand there and watch us like we're some kind of damn movie," one said.

Nat laughed. "That's not a bad idea."

I poured a small portion of soup into my bowl and sat next to Nat, leaning against him slightly. He wrapped an arm around me briefly, then started eating. His display of affection didn't fool me. It wasn't forgiveness. But feeding his belief that I needed him and loved him helped blunt some of his anger. Sometimes.

"You did an amazing job with the supplies," I said. "This is much better than anything we would have had in that hellhole." The word was bitter in my mouth. Tenacity had been a haven.

"This is the first haul from that bitch's house," Nat said. "The guy was a cocky son of a bitch who got what he deserved, but he sure knew how to pick supplies." Nat paused with the spoon partway to his mouth. "We'll need to go back there. It's not right that there was no consequence for what she and her man did to Wayne. And we get kicked out for standing up for ourselves? No, that's not right, not at all."

The other men made sounds of agreement.

"Don't you think that's not, right?" Nat asked, looking at me.

"No, it's not right at all," I said quickly, knowing it was already too late. "Can I get you more soup?"

His gaze swept over my face.

"No. I'm not hungry for food anymore. Let's go cuddle, Shelby."

He set his bowl down and stood, holding out a hand to me. The men around us smirked and chuckled, thinking they knew what Nat had in mind. They didn't. Nat was discreet with what he did to me.

I took his hand, trying not to tremble, and let him lead me to the tent. My gaze strayed to the iron balcony, and I briefly thought of running. It wouldn't do any good. I had nowhere to go. Nowhere that Nat wouldn't come looking for me. My stomach twisted with the knowledge, and I hoped Matt and June would be smart enough to watch for Nat's retaliation in the days to come.

The fey near the tree moved, catching my attention.

"I think he's leaving," I said, hoping for a last-minute distraction.

"Good," Nat said.

My feet dragged.

"Please, Nat," I whispered, unable to stop myself.

"In the tent, Shelby."

The damn tears let loose without my permission, and I sniffled. His hand tightened around mine, and he hauled me to the orange tent, ignoring any hint of resistance as he shoved me inside. I fell to my knees on a sleeping bag. The sound of the zipper pierced the space.

"I was so worried about you, Shelby-baby, when I came to, bound and gagged. All I could think of was how we'd left you to keep watch. What could have happened to my wife to stop her from calling out a warning? It must have been bad."

He pushed me down, turning me so we faced each other, and his hands circled my throat.

"Was it bad, baby? How did they hurt you?"

"Please, Nat. Don't do this," I rasped. He pulled back and hit my stomach. I grunted in pain but didn't fight him as he ripped open the button of my jeans. Fighting back always made it worse.

He yanked the material down my legs, keeping me pinned with a hand on my throat.

"Not a new mark on you," he murmured. He lifted his gaze to mine. "I'm so glad you're safe, baby."

I closed my eyes and focused on the sensation of the tear rolling down my cheek. A soft sob escaped me, and he leaned in and kissed me roughly.

"I love you, Shelby. You're everything to me."

He shoved my underwear down and finally released me to unbutton his pants.

"Shit!" someone yelled from outside the tent.

I opened my eyes and looked up at Nat. He knelt above me, his dick peeking out from his pants and his head tipped to the side as he listened. A scuffle of noise came from outside the tent, then silence.

Nat lifted his finger to his lips and reached over for the gun he'd set to the side. Trembling beneath him, I wasn't sure what to hope for. If an infected was out there, we were both as good as dead. But maybe dead wouldn't be so bad. Another muffled sob escaped me.

The tent ripped open above Nat's head, and he disappeared.

I scrambled to pull up my underwear and pants. When I stood in the shredded opening, I had a clear view of the balcony. All of the men who'd been eating only moments ago now lay in a pile of bodies. Bodies that still had their heads.

My wide gaze swung to the fey standing nearby. An unconscious Nat dangled from his hand, and the sight of my husband's slack face did some crazy things to me. I wanted to crow and laugh and point, but I also wanted to beg the fey not to hurt him. Sparing Nat some pain might spare me pain.

I opened my mouth to say something, but nothing came out.

The fey's green and yellow eyes skimmed over me as he tossed Nat to the side. I jumped slightly and started to shake.

"What do you want? Why did you hurt them?" I asked.

The fey blinked at me.

"He hurt you."

My face heated, and I clasped my hands in front of me.

"What do you mean?"

"He hit you and you cried." He held out his hand to me.

"You don't have to stay with them. I will take you somewhere safe."

I couldn't keep the surprise from my face as I stared at the fey's large, grey hand. It took a moment for what he was saying to sink in. Leave Nat.

"He won't let me leave."

"He doesn't have a choice. You do," the fey said, his voice almost angry. "Do you want to stay with the humans, or do you want to leave?"

I stared at his grey palm, open and waiting. If I stayed, I would endure a lifetime as Nat's punching bag and worse. Even though I'd been with him for less than a year, it already felt like I'd spent an eternity with him, and I was already so tired. Tired of the fear. Tired of the pain. Tired of the shame. Yet, I didn't have a choice.

Lifting my gaze, I locked eyes with the fey. His green-yellow gaze held mine, so alien and closed off.

"You don't understand. If I leave with you, he'll follow. He'll try to hurt you or me or whoever. He won't let me go. Ever."

The fey's gaze flicked to Nat.

"He tried to hurt me last night, but it didn't work. Trust me to keep you safe, Shelby. No one will ever hurt you again."

I wanted that. Desperately. But I knew what accepting the offer would do. It would put the fey, Matt, and everyone in Tenacity within Nat's crosshairs.

"What's your name?" I asked.

"Turik."

"Turik, I don't want anyone to be hurt because of me."

"No one will be."

"They will," I said, being honest. "But I want you to

remember this moment. That I warned you my selfish choice would put people in danger."

Yet, it was a choice I made regardless of the risks when I placed my hand in Turik's, and his fingers closed around mine. I just couldn't stay with Nat for a minute more.

"Wanting safety and kindness isn't selfish, Shelby. Asking you to live in fear is."

A shaky exhale escaped me.

"Then take me somewhere safe. Please. I'm tired of living in fear." I swallowed back the tears that wanted to fall, and I hoped I hadn't just damned us both.

CHAPTER THREE

ONE OF THE MEN GROANED, ADDING ANOTHER LEVEL OF apprehension to my decision.

"May I carry you?" Turik asked.

I nodded, desperate to leave quickly now that I'd decided. Turik didn't feel the same need to rush. He approached me cautiously like he was waiting for me to lash out at him. When I did nothing, he carefully lifted me into his arms.

This wasn't my first time accepting a fey ride. I knew what to expect. The strength in his hard arms. The heat radiating from his torso. The way he held me a little too close. I didn't mind any of it. I just wished he would do something more than stare down at me. We needed to go.

I shifted impatiently in his arms.

"Am I hurting you?" he asked.

I shook my head as my gaze flicked to the pile of bodies. One of them was moving.

"We need to go now," I whispered urgently.

"Hold on." That was the only warning I got before he ran and jumped off the balcony.

A scream rose in my throat, but I choked on it a second later when we landed with a jolt.

"You are safe," Turik said, taking off at a sprint, the speed of which had my eyes watering.

I tucked my face against his chest and let him do what he and his kind did best aside from killing infected—ensuring healthy humans stayed healthy. Especially the women. We were damn near sacred to them. So I held onto him as he ran exceptionally fast through the trees.

A few moans echoed in the distance, letting me know we weren't alone in the woods. But I didn't feel the same level of worry that I'd felt earlier when walking away from Tenacity. I knew Turik wouldn't let anything happen to me. Not only was he faster and stronger than a human, but his kind also didn't have a vindictive bone in their bodies.

The fey's gentle souls were why other humans treated them even more cruelly than we did each other. The fey's differences alienated them when all they wanted was acceptance. Turik's words about safety and kindness hit me a second time as I realized he might have been talking about himself too.

I burrowed into his warmth and tried not to think for the next several minutes. Thinking led to doubt and guilt, and I couldn't afford either. For better or worse, I had made a decision. Only time would tell if it was the right one.

The sudden lurch in my stomach indicated another jump and had me lifting my head just as Turik landed inside a very familiar recycled vehicle wall. I hadn't given a thought to where he planned to take me. Anywhere away from Nat would have been good. Anywhere other than the community we'd been kicked out of just that morning.

"I can't be here," I said in a panic. "I was exiled."

"Matt and June said you couldn't live in Tenacity. They didn't say you couldn't live in Tolerance."

"It's the same thing, Turik. I can't be here."

He ignored me and kept walking while I scanned the unfamiliar houses for opening doors.

"Please, Turik. I had to suffer the shame of being kicked out once and never want to go through that again."

"You won't. No one will make you leave." His arms tightened fractionally around me, and I wondered if he was trying to reassure himself or me.

I glanced at the houses again, but didn't see any sign of people. Not a fey or a human. I'd held the impression that Tolerance was just as packed—with fey—as Tenacity had been with humans.

"Where is everyone?" I asked in a hush.

He grunted, which I knew meant he didn't know, and it wasn't reassuring. The absence of people increased the disquiet and insecurity I felt. Being in his arms helped take the edge off of some of it, though. I'd always found the fey presence comforting rather than disturbing, not that I'd ever let anyone know that.

Turik turned down another quiet side street and walked us to a beautiful two-story house with immaculate landscaping. Shifting my weight to one arm, he used the other to let us in.

The home was warm but just as quiet as the rest of the town.

"Do you live here?" I asked when he closed the door behind us but made no move to put me down.

"Yes."

"Alone?"

"No. Vorx and I share this place. There is enough room for us."

I looked around the open living room and kitchen and agreed. "This house looks big enough for a family of eight. Is this where I'll be staying?" I didn't want to assume or get my hopes up. It was a well-kept house. Comfortable furniture accented with colorful throw pillows offset the clean walls painted in muted, neutral tones. Much nicer than the house we'd been staying in at Tenacity, especially since there were only two other people in this one.

"Yes, you can stay here with me."

"And Vorx?"

"Yes."

I studied the comfortable couch and pretty decorations. A blue vase with teal swirls on a shelf near the television caught my eye. It was pretty. But more than that, it was now probably irreplaceable.

"Nat will try to find me, Turik. And he will wreck everything here if he gets the chance."

Turik grunted, and I exhaled slowly. I didn't know what else I could say or do to help him understand the danger I was putting him in. Oh, I knew the fey could protect themselves. That Turik had climbed up to the third-story balcony and knocked all the men out proved he was more than adept at dealing with humans. But Nat wouldn't fight fair.

Nat wouldn't come at the fey in the open. He'd ensure he had the advantage, and he wouldn't care how many people he hurt or what he destroyed to get the result he wanted...which was all the fey dead and me back by his side.

My stomach churned at the thought. If Nat succeeded, everything I'd suffered at his hands prior to this would seem like a walk in the park compared to what he would do to me.

Pushing those thoughts aside, I focused on the present. Nat

wasn't here yet, and I was still safely under the protection of Turik.

I looked up at him and found his green and yellow gaze locked on me. His vertical pupils were so large they almost looked round. I knew he was attracted to me. It didn't mean much, though. The fey adored human females because they didn't have any females of their own. My gender was a complete mystery to them. I couldn't even count the number of times one of them had asked me if they could see my undercarriage.

"If I'm going to live here, maybe you should show me around. And let me walk." He didn't make any move to put me down, and I suppressed a defeated sigh. "I know what you want from me, Turik. But I am still married."

His gaze shifted to my hand as he slowly lowered me to my own feet.

"Terri's first husband removed her ring and said they were no longer married. You can remove your ring and tell Nat he is not your husband. Brooke says that's the only way to divorce now."

Terri was the now-ex-wife of one of Nat's friends. She'd started trading with the fey, which had upset her husband and led to him kicking her out of their place. I'd heard him vent to Nat about how he'd tried taking her ring so that everyone would know she wasn't with him anymore.

Brooke had been one of Terri's housemates who'd also come to live in Tolerance. She'd been single then, but she had a good point. Considering there wasn't much of the world left, I didn't suppose there was any better way to divorce someone than removing the rings and announcing it.

Not that the absence of the bands around my finger would help me in any way.

"I can remove the rings and say I'm not married all I want, but it won't change how Nat views me. He will always say I'm his."

Turik shook his head and lifted my hand.

"You have a choice, too. And a voice. You both have to want to stay married. My brothers will know your choice if you remove this ring."

I looked down at my wedding band and diamond engagement ring. If I removed them, I would be single in the eyes of the fey—single and fair game for open pursuit. If I kept them on, I knew the fey would still protect me, but I would be off limits. More importantly, when Nat came for me, he would see the rings and know I hadn't turned my back on him. It might spare me a little.

I didn't want to be spared. I wanted to be done. Done with the fear and the cowering. Done with the sleepless nights and the pain. Especially the pain.

Slowly, I tugged the rings from my finger and handed them to Turik.

"Because of this, he will kill me when he finds me."

"Never," Turik said fiercely, closing his fingers around the rings.

I met his gaze, saw his determination, and felt pity for him. At some point, Nat would get to me, and Turik would be the one to suffer because he was putting his hopes and dreams on the wrong woman.

Story of my life.

CHAPTER FOUR

Turik's home was pristine like it came straight out of a magazine. However, of the five bedrooms, only two of them had beds. Apparently, there was a clean mattress shortage. But not toiletries. All three bathrooms were fully stocked. The house even boasted a firepit and patio furniture out on a back deck that begged for entertaining.

The only room that was less than spotless was the den. It had pieces of paper all over the desk. The random squiggly drawings didn't depict anything I could identify, and I briefly wondered what the subject was supposed to be. I didn't ask, though. I didn't want to offend Turik.

"This place is beyond beautiful," I said when he concluded the tour in the kitchen. "You and Vorx are lucky to live here."

He grunted, his gaze never leaving my face.

My brief interactions with the fey had strictly revolved around gathering supplies. I hadn't spoken to them more than necessary or shown any interest in conversations regarding them. It wouldn't have been healthy for me. But I couldn't continue my ignorance if I meant to live with them.

"I don't know a lot about the fey," I said. "I know you came from some caves that were exposed during the earthquakes a few months back and that you didn't have women or children with you."

"That is all true." His gaze dipped to my midsection. "Do you like children?"

The random question shot a bolt of panic through me, which I managed to keep off my expression.

"I like kids just fine, I guess." I used to have that whole white-picket-fence dream before I married Nat. He quickly showed me that children would never survive.

I moved to the couch and made myself comfortable. Turik took the nearby chair. He continued to observe my every move with a level of scrutiny that reminded me of Nat, and it made me nervous. I talked too much when I was nervous.

"Someone told me that the fey couldn't die in the caves but that you can up here. Is that true too?" I asked. It was a fact that Nat had been desperate to prove and one I hoped wasn't true.

"Yes, and no," Turik said. "We could die in the caves but were always reborn in the resurrection pools. We didn't understand that wouldn't remain the same once we were on the surface."

"How many times were you reborn?" I asked.

"Many."

"So you're really old, then?"

He frowned thoughtfully for a moment.

"I don't know. Our days and nights weren't the same as they are here. There was no sun to measure our time. Only the crystals lit the darkness. And the hours each cave remained lit were different." He shrugged slightly. "Mya thinks we were in the caves for thousands of years. Perhaps even hundreds of thousands."

"Wow. That's a lot." I studied his chiseled physique for a moment. He was as largely built as the rest of them—a good foot and a half taller than myself—with biceps the size of my head. His grey skin was smooth perfection. Not a wrinkle in sight. Except for laugh lines around his mouth and eyes.

I met his gaze, seeing him, the individual. He had the hint of a divot in his cheek that I would bet turned into a dimple with a full smile. The evidence of his capacity for humor didn't take away from his strength; it simply added to his deadly charm.

"You sure don't look that old," I said, picking up the conversation again. "I would have guessed late twenties, early thirties at best. Your age sure doesn't slow you down either. I've seen how strong and fast the fey are. It must be disconcerting to be around people who are so fragile in comparison."

His expression shifted to one of surprise, and he quickly leaned forward, bracing his elbows on his knees.

"Yes. The stupid ones break so easily. Their heads come right off. I was extra careful when I put the men with you to sleep, but many of them will wake with headaches." He shook his head. "Shax is worried about the baby. Angel says he will be fine, but he's played with Timmy and Savvy. They fall and bleed from hitting the ground. They sneeze, and they cry. I want children, but I don't want children."

He was so emphatic that a small smile curved my lips before I could smother it. He smiled in return, humor lighting his expression and making him more handsome.

I smothered that thought and focused on our conversation.

"I understand what you're saying. Kids are a lot of work and responsibility. A lot to care for." And that was why I'd had an IUD put in shortly after Nat and I had gotten married. I couldn't protect myself. How would I have ever been able to protect a baby? Especially when Nat really enjoyed hitting me in the stomach.

My gaze drifted to my empty left hand while my thoughts drifted to those darker moments. Fear curled inside of me, and I fisted my fingers.

There was no going back now. Only forward.

"What else is different about the surface?" I asked to distract myself from thoughts of Nat.

"Females," Turik said immediately. "They look different. They talk different. They think different. They are fun to watch but cry and run away all the time." I heard a hint of annoyance in his tone at the end. But not anger.

"I suppose it does seem like that. But I think we're getting used to our differences and aren't running quite as much. The pointed ears were a little shocking in the beginning." I tucked my hair behind my ear and turned my head slightly. "Weren't our small ears disturbing when you first saw us?"

He snorted.

"I didn't see ears. I saw chest mounds and heard about female pussies. A hole where your cock should be is more disturbing than an ear."

A laugh ripped from me. "I guess I never thought of it that way. The fixation makes a bit more sense now."

"Is there truly nothing there but a hole covered by hair?"

"Uh...I mean, there's no penis, if that's what you're asking."

"Can I see?"

Another laugh escaped me. "No. And asking to see a woman's privates probably is what sends us running away."

He grunted and leaned back in his chair.

"Solin drew Brooke's pussy to show us what it looks like, but Brooke said it was a private picture and he shouldn't share it. Ghua had magazines with pictures of pussies, but Eden and Mya burned them all. I don't think pussies are real." He crossed his arms and gave me a smug look. "I think you have chest mounds and a small cock."

"If you're hoping I'm going to drop my pants and prove you wrong, it's not going to happen. I'm not the show-and-tell type."

A brief expression of disappointment danced over his features as he grunted and uncrossed his arms. However, it disappeared as quickly as it had appeared. I wasn't sure what to think of that since Nat often hid what he was actually feeling behind his polite mask.

"Are you hungry?" Turik asked abruptly. "Vorx and I have plenty of food."

He stood and went to the kitchen. Packages, canned goods, and bags filled each cupboard he opened. Like a moth drawn to a flame, I stood and drifted closer to him—and the food. The abundance stunned me.

"Are those cheese curls?" I asked, unable to look away from the bag. I couldn't remember the last time I'd enjoyed the snack. Saliva pooled in my mouth.

No matter how desperately I wanted to gorge on the snack, though, I kept my hands at my sides and the hope off my face. It wasn't my food to take.

Turik removed and opened the bag before handing the whole thing to me. I accepted with a smile of thanks, and he watched closely as I took one curl out and popped it into my mouth. The processed cheddar flavor hit my tongue, and I groaned.

"I know these are full of chemicals and preservatives and aren't good for me, but I missed them so much. It's been ages."

I helped myself to another one, savoring the taste while looking at the supplies Turik and his roommate had accumulated. I could imagine the jealousy and resentment that many of the people in Tenacity would show if they saw this. Especially one particular group of people.

"If Nat had known how much food was here, he would have caused trouble."

"He did cause trouble," Turik said. "And it didn't help him gain more food. He lost his chance with females. Nat isn't smart. Or scary. You're safe here. Do you want to try a new bag?"

I smiled at Turik's blunt honesty and interpretation of what had happened.

"No, these are perfect for now. I wouldn't mind a glass of water to go with it, though."

He opened another cupboard, and instead of handing me the glass, he filled it for me and gestured that I should sit at the counter.

"You don't have to wait on me," I said even as I sat. "I can get my own water."

"I want to do things for you. I want you to enjoy living here so you stay."

"Where else do you think I would go?"

"To live with one of my brothers."

I frowned slightly and munched on another cheese curl as I tried to understand how Turik might see our arrangement.

"I don't plan on going anywhere. You're the one who offered me somewhere safe to stay despite the part I played in stealing food and my exile for it. Your brothers might not be so forgiving. However, you do bring up a good point. Neither of us knows what to expect with this arrangement. So let's lay it out.

"How is this going to work with me living here, Turik? What are my responsibilities? How can I be a contributing member of this house and the community?"

He considered me for a thoughtful moment.

"Brooke draws. Angel lets us feel the baby move inside of her and teaches us how to make women feel good with our hands. Eden lets Ghua lick her pussy. Brenna teaches the other women how to fight. Emily comes up with ideas to show females that the fey are nice and would make good husbands. Mary likes to look at our cocks, but James says we shouldn't let her see them anymore. Hannah—"

"Hold up. Who is Mary? And should I be concerned that you only listed like two things that weren't related to sex in some way?"

"Mya says that Mary is a grandma and old and fragile. We have to be careful with elderly humans. Mary will feed us and let anyone without a house take a shower in her home. James is Mary's husband. He says seeing too many cocks in one day isn't good for Mary's heart, so my brothers take turns showering there.

"And sex is an excellent way to contribute. If you choose to have sex with me, you will be contributing to this house and the community. You can ride my face like a pony if you want."

I snapped my mouth closed, unsure when, during all that, it had fallen open.

"I don't know where you heard that turn of phrase, but it's not exactly nice. It's like asking a woman to see her privates. More likely to send her running than to get a 'yes,' okay?"

He grunted, his annoyance briefly showing before he shifted his focus to the cabinets for a moment.

"I just want to have a female of my own. I want to feed her and protect her and hold her while she sleeps. I want to give her little kisses when she's sad and see her smile when she's happy. Why do females keep wanting to run away from males who only want to give?"

CHAPTER FIVE

I STUDIED TURIK'S EARNEST EXPRESSION AND FELT MY OPINION OF the fey shift. The men came across as slightly naïve in most conversations. Yet, they had a way of seeing into the heart of things that really brought clarity to a situation.

Why *were* women so reluctant to let the fey care for them? Yes, these huge males wanted romantic relationships. So what? So did half the human population.

The fey were strong, dependable, and non-violent to females. Their unique eyes, ears, and skin coloring aside, there wasn't a single good reason to run from them. Except for, perhaps, a lack of interest in hooking up with any man at the moment.

"I don't have a good answer for you," I said. "But I can tell you that, for me specifically, having just removed Nat's ring, I'm not ready for the type of relationship you want. I didn't like how Nat...cared for me and need some time to move past that. Which means I'm not interested in having sex with anyone right now."

"We don't need to have sex. I would be happy to lick your pussy until you make happy sounds."

A flush of heat rocketed through me.

"No. I'm not ready for that either," I managed.

"What about small kisses on your face?"

"I think that's something we would need to work up to. Can we maybe just start with being friends?"

That suggestion would have been a death knell for most other men, but Turik didn't seem the least put out by it.

"Okay. What do friends do?"

"They talk to each other like we're doing. Or get each other something to drink or make a meal for each other, like we're doing now. But without any expectation of sexual compensation."

"Yes, I can do that. I will feed you and protect you. Can I hold you while you sleep too?"

"Um, maybe just not yet. But we should probably talk about sleeping arrangements. I'm happy to take the couch and look for another mattress—"

He was already shaking his head, his easy-going expression gone.

"My bed is big. We can both sleep on it."

The determined light in his eyes told me he wouldn't easily bend to my way of thinking. I also knew how much the fey valued consent and that I wouldn't need to worry about being violated while I slept.

A night without fear of abuse would be a pleasant change of pace.

"You know what? That's fine," I said.

His answering smile was so wide it showed his back molars

and his very pointed canines. Along with the dimple I'd suspected he possessed. He truly was a handsome man, and I was glad I'd given him some small measure of joy after all he'd already done for me. Who knew how much he would have in the future?

"Back to how to contribute," I said. "I'd like to do more than just live here. Do you go on daily supply runs? Even though I'm not living in Tenacity, maybe I could go on supply runs and help contribute to their stock."

Turik considered it for a moment.

"I will speak to Mya and Drav and let them know you would like to help in some way. They will have suggestions."

The idea of Turik going to Tolerance's leaders and admitting he'd taken me in made me feel a little queasy. They'd probably demand that I leave right away. But wasn't getting kicked out now better than settling in and loving this place? I wasn't sure I could cope with the sting of dismissal to that degree again.

"Yeah, talking to Mya and Drav is probably a good idea. Should we go see them now?"

Turik glanced at the front door and shook his head.

"I can hear my brothers returning. We will wait for Vorx and find out what happened while I was gone."

Willing to extend my visit just a little longer, I munched while we waited. However, I only managed a handful more of the snack before the front door opened. Another fey Turik's size entered the house. His gaze immediately found mine, and he hesitated for a fraction of a second before closing the door.

"Why is Shelby here?" he asked.

My face flushed with shame, and I quickly put down the cheese curls. I'd known I wouldn't be welcome, but damn, it hurt. I opened my mouth to say I would go, but Turik answered first.

"She removed her rings and asked to live somewhere safe. I brought her here to live with us. She isn't ready for sex but said I could feed and protect her. Soon I will hold her while she sleeps."

Dumbfounded, I tore my gaze from the fey I assumed was Vorx to stare at Turik.

"She doesn't mind if you continue to live here with us," Turik added.

My mouth dropped open at Turik's audacity, and I glanced at Vorx.

"It's your house, Vorx," I said quickly. "I—"

"Groth enjoys living with Azio and Terri. He rubbed Terri's boobs when she had her period and listened to them make their baby. I will enjoy doing both if you decide to choose Turik."

"Oh... that's not what I—" I took a calming breath and started over. "I appreciate that you're both willing to let me stay here. Truly. I'm just looking for a safe place to sleep and would like to contribute in some small, non-sexual way. That's all."

"Where were you?" Turik asked, changing the subject.

"Much has happened since dawn," Vorx said as he joined us in the kitchen. "Uan and our brothers have returned. The stupid ones followed them here and bit Adam.

"Seeing Adam hurt June's heart, but Tor is helping her. They will move back to Tenacity to assist Matt with changing things there, now that the angry ones are gone. And Drav wants to send out scouts to find a location for a new town so the rest of our brothers can have homes too. I was going to go, but now I'll stay."

That was by far the most I'd heard one of them say at one time. And I'd probably only understood about a third of it.

"Someone was bitten?" I asked.

"Yes. The human man that was beaten in Tenacity."

Guilt hit me hard because I knew exactly who June and Adam were. It was Nat's fault that Adam had been beaten.

"The infected stole him on the way home from our caves," Vorx continued. "They brought him here and bit him. No one understands why." He shrugged. "The infected don't do smart things."

"Don't they?" I asked. "They know to hide when we go out for supplies and wait to spring their traps. And they seem to know they can't turn you fey because they never try to go after you. I mean, they do come at you, but it's like they're just trying to figure out how to get through you to get to us humans. At least, that's how it seems to me since, once we're safely out of reach, they tend to give up and retreat."

Turik and Vorx exchanged an indecipherable look.

"I wasn't trying to be contradictory," I said, fumbling to take back whatever I'd said to cause their reaction. "Sorry."

"We like hearing your thoughts," Turik said. "And you may be right."

"I'll mention it to Ryan before he goes out to help scout for a new location," Vorx said.

"Does he need help with that?" I asked quickly. "I'd like to volunteer if he does."

I wasn't keen on leaving the safety of the wall, especially to wander around the countryside without the protection of a supply truck and a lot of fey. But helping establish a new safe zone might redeem me in a few people's eyes. And it would definitely contribute to the wellbeing of the people in the current safe zones.

"I will ask Ryan," Vorx said.

But he didn't move to leave. Instead, he stared at me.

Uncomfortable but trying not to show it, I waited for him to say something more. When he didn't, I glanced at Turik, who was also watching me. He nudged the bag of cheese curls, prodding me to keep eating.

"No, thank you," I said as politely as possible.

I glanced at the light coming in through the windows. Though we still had a few hours before dark, it wasn't likely anyone would scout for new locations today. However, that did give us time to make arrangements for tomorrow.

"Can we talk to Ryan today?" I asked, closing the snack bag and setting it aside. "And Mya and Drav? I'd sleep better knowing I'm allowed to stay here and have a way to offer something in return."

Turik stood and put the bag away.

"You are allowed here," Turik said firmly. "But we will go so you can hear it from Drav and Mya."

"Thank you."

Wishing I had Turik's confidence, I followed the pair to the door and quickly put on my shoes and jacket. After my part in what had happened in Tenacity, the people of Tolerance had no reason to let me remain here. Hopefully, my willingness to help establish a new safe zone would give them one.

Tolerance no longer felt like a ghost town when we left the house. Fey roamed the streets and walked between dwellings. A few humans loitered on porches, too. Groups paused on sidewalks to chat, and the murmur of conversation hummed in the air.

The people who saw us nodded in passing. The fey stared at me, and I offered pained smiles in return, knowing full well that they were probably wondering what I, the wife of the fey-hater, was doing in their town.

It didn't take us long to reach the house Turik said belonged to Mya and Drav. He knocked on the door, and I wiped my damp palms on my jeans.

The large fey who opened the door glanced at me first, then Turik.

"Shelby thinks we do not want her here and would like to speak with you and Mya."

My cheeks heated as I endured Drav's unblinking focus, and I wished that Turik would have been a little less blunt about our reason for being there.

"Every female is wanted," Drav said after an extended pause. Then he gave credence to his words by opening the door wider so we could enter.

Feeling vulnerable and exposed, I entered his home.

"Mya is in the kitchen."

The fey hung back, leaving me to make my way to the woman who was essentially in charge of all the fey. The young brunette frosted cookies on the counter near the stove. At the sound of my approach, she looked up with a questioning smile.

"Hi. I'm Shelby."

"Ah. Shelby." Her smile disappeared. "June told me about you. Come have a seat."

CHAPTER SIX

SHAME BURNED INSIDE OF ME. WHILE JUNE HAD BEEN FORGIVING about my part in breaking into her home and stealing her food, I'd known others wouldn't feel the same way. Yet, experiencing that anger still stung painfully.

"Turik offered me somewhere safe to stay. I didn't know he meant to bring me to Tolerance," I said, speaking in a rush as I sat at the table. "And I understand why I shouldn't be here. But Vorx mentioned that the fey are looking to set up a new place. Is there any possibility that I could help find one and maybe earn a second chance there?"

"Why did Turik offer you somewhere to stay? I thought you left with your husband."

"He hit her," Turik said from behind me. "She begged him not to and cried."

Mya's gaze never wavered from mine, and I clutched my hands in my lap, letting my nails bite into my palms to keep my humiliation from showing.

"So you left your husband?" she asked.

"She removed his rings," Turik said. "He is no longer her husband."

I could feel the flush creeping into my cheeks but refused to look away. And I was glad I didn't when I witnessed the softening in Mya's expression.

"Good for you," she said, surprising me. "That couldn't have been easy."

She took a seat at the table and slid a plate with a cookie in front of me. I couldn't make myself reach for the treat. My hands were shaking too much.

"I don't think there's much in life that is easy," I said instead.

"Oh, I agree with you there." She set her cookie down and leaned forward in her chair. "Listen, you know that Matt and June didn't want to exile you with the others. They understood you were being coerced. If Turik's fine with taking you in, you're welcome to stay here, and Ryan wouldn't mind some help looking for a Tolerance two-point-oh if you're willing. But staying here isn't contingent on that.

"This is your second chance. Don't steal, don't cause trouble, and you have a home here. It's that simple."

My nails bit into my hands even harder.

"I don't want to cause trouble, but it might follow me here."

"You mean your ex-husband."

"Removing that ring won't mean anything to him. In his mind, I'm still his wife."

She exhaled deeply and glanced over my shoulder.

"She thinks Nat is going to come looking for her. Make sure the fey keep an eye out for him and his men. They aren't welcome here and should be removed if they show up." She focused on me once more. "The fey won't let him near you again. And if any of those men cause trouble, you're not to blame for it. They're making their own choices. Now, eat that cookie and tell me if I have a future as a baker. I need to figure out my occupation here."

"I thought you were the leader," I said, picking up the cookie.

"Temporary only. Once Molev gets back, I'll happily return to consultant mode and be a full-time whatever this place needs."

"A mother," Drav said.

She rolled her eyes at him.

"Seriously, I'll be lucky if I can hold this baby long enough to breastfeed it. All your brothers will be begging to babysit. Having an occupation is a good thing. It will give me a sense of purpose."

He grunted, and she grinned at me.

"If he had his way, my purpose would be a baby PEZ dispenser."

"They all seem to have that singular thought," I said before taking a bite of the peanut butter cookie.

"They do. Well, how is it? Good or amazing?. Be honest."

I swallowed and gave her a slight shrug.

"It's good. Sorry."

"No, it's okay. I knew finding an occupation wouldn't be easy. Sewing is next. Ryan found a few sewing machines, and my mom is going to give a couple of us lessons. She's hoping there might be a natural in the group. I really hope that's not me."

As she continued to talk about all the career options Tolerance offered, I slowly relaxed. She truly didn't seem to care about my past and invited me to join in on their quest to make Tolerance more self-sustaining.

"I've always had a bit of a green thumb," I admitted. "Maybe once the weather warms, I can help with planting some of those seeds you mentioned."

"Farming is a noble occupation," she said with a nod. "And I sure do like eating."

"Same. Thank you for this. The chance and the conversation. Since it's not time to plant anything yet, I think I'll still talk to Ryan about his plans about scouting for a new place."

"He'll appreciate the help."

I breathed a little easier when we left Mya and Drav's house just before dark. Turik and Vorx walked beside me as we made our way to Ryan's place. An older gentleman I recalled from my last supply run answered our knock.

"Hi, Dad," Turik said. "Is Ryan here?"

"Yep. Come on in."

As we followed him inside, I appreciatively inhaled the scent of roasting meat.

"Any chance you boys are going to help me with the supply run tomorrow?" the man asked, shutting the door behind us.

"Shelby wants to help Ryan," Vorx said. "Sorry, Dad." The big fey sympathetically patted the man on the back.

The man's gaze shifted to me. "Nice to see you again, Shelby." He held out his hand. "I don't think we've been officially introduced. I'm Richard. Ryan and Mya's father."

I shook his hand, trying to quell my hesitation. Did he know I'd been exiled from Tenacity?

"Ryan and I were in the den, studying the maps for tomorrow. I know he'd love some input."

We followed him into the main part of the house. It was an open, sprawling space that connected the living room, kitchen, and dining room with an arched opening to a den.

"Vorx and Turik, I hope you boys are here for dinner," a woman said from the kitchen. "That roast Gyrik found is big enough to feed ten people."

Instead of answering her, Turik looked at me. The woman chuckled at my confusion.

"He's waiting for you to decide. I have a roast with potatoes and carrots, and there's plenty for everyone."

My mouth started salivating at the thought of eating a real meal. I'd been living on stews and soups for months.

"I can't say no to that," I said honestly. "Thank you for the invitation."

She waved away my thanks.

"All I did was cook it. These boys do all the work finding it. Go on in by Ryan. Dinner won't be ready for another hour."

Ryan sat at a large, dark table with several chairs around it. Maps covered the surface.

"I miss technology," Ryan said when we entered. At only eighteen, he was the brains behind all the groups that left to scavenge supplies. The toll of that responsibility showed in his messy hair and the slump of his shoulders.

"Do you know how easy it would be to search a map online? We'd have current aerial shots of all the subdivisions in the area. These maps have to be at least a decade old. This subdivision isn't even on any of them."

"Yeah, old-time map makers would have a hard time keeping up with all the subdivisions going in around here. Around any small town close to a major highway, really. People like living in rural locations with access to the conveniences found in a big city."

Ryan stared at me for a moment.

"Shelby, I could kiss you."

"Shelby is not ready for kisses. And when she is, you will not give her any." The slow way Turik delivered those words and how he crossed his arms carried a hint of menace.

Ryan just grinned.

"I can see why Garrett gets jumpy. Turik, I promise it would be a brother kiss if I ever give her one, and it was more of an expression than anything since she just gave us the answer we needed."

"I did?" I asked as Turik grunted and uncrossed his arms.

"You did," Ryan said. "We need to look for small towns near major highways. Ones far enough from the closest city so light and sound won't draw in infected."

"And something far enough from the highway that the lights won't draw unwanted people in," I said, thinking of Nat and his men.

Ryan nodded, his gaze already sweeping over the maps in front of him. I didn't hesitate to pull up a chair and join him in looking at the area around Warrensburg. Within an hour, we had several spots circled as locations that would work if subdivisions existed there.

"It's still all guesswork, but at least it's guesswork with possibility," Ryan said, leaning back. "I'm glad you showed up when you did. I was ready to pull my hair out." He paused and gave us a sheepish smile. "I should have probably asked if there was something you needed before pulling you into my map madness."

"We came for this," I said, indicating the maps. "I wanted to offer my help tomorrow, scouting for new places."

"Really? Garrett and Dad are taking over the supply run so I can go out with a group of fey and scout. If you're willing to scout too, that'll cut our search time in half."

"I'm willing," I said.

"That's great. Thank you. With the new arrivals, we'll have plenty of fey to split up into two groups. We might even manage three groups if Eden or Brenna are willing to go out." He stood and started folding the maps. "I'm going to go—"

"Sit yourself at the table for the meal your mother made?" Julie finished from the other room.

Ryan deflated a little, then grinned.

"Exactly that, Mom. You're a true mind reader."

We left the maps and joined Ryan and his parents for the most filling dinner I'd had in ages. The roast melted in my mouth like butter. Paired with canned potatoes and carrots? I was in heaven.

"This is the best meal I've eaten in months," I said when I couldn't take another bite. "Thank you for sharing it with me."

"It was a pleasure having you. Stop by any time you don't want to cook. There's always a meal here." The open welcome they'd all shown humbled me, and I said a heartfelt goodbye after helping clean up.

"Get some quality sleep," Ryan said at the door. "Tomorrow's going to be a long day."

I almost laughed at that, unable to see how the next day could be longer than the current one. How many hours of sleep had I managed last night before Nat woke me to help break into June's place? Three? Maybe four? After being caught, there'd been too much fear to allow for sleep. Fear of Nat's retribution. Fear of leaving the safety of Tenacity.

As Vorx, Turik, and I walked back to their place, the events of the day tumbled through my head. The long, terrifying walk through the woods. Nat's punishment. My rescue.

Those memories felt like they belonged to a different person —one who wasn't well-fed and safely sandwiched between two fey.

That thought brought back the reality of my situation. I was finally free, and the possibility that I could go to sleep without fear of being woken up by a fist in the middle of the night filled me with elation.

"I hope you smile like that when you sleep tonight," Turik said.

"Why?" I asked, confused.

"It will make stroking his cock while he watches you more enjoyable," Vorx said with a smirk.

I stumbled a step, and my gaze flew to Turik's.

CHAPTER SEVEN

"You're going to do what?" The question came out less of a demand and more of a horrified whisper.

The tips of Turik's ears darkened slightly in the glow of the car lights illuminating the distant wall. But he didn't stammer an excuse to play off Vorx's comment. He freaking admitted it, although uncertainly.

"Stroke my cock while I watch you sleep?"

Whatever he saw on my face had him quickly adding, "But I will imagine your smile means you want me as much as I want you."

As if that made it better. Yet, after our talk this afternoon, his response did soften my reaction to the situation.

"Turik, that's a really creepy thing to say."

"It's creepy to dream of you wanting me as much as I want you?"

"It's creepy to tell a woman you're going to masturbate while you watch her sleep. I don't want you watching me sleep. And I definitely don't want you watching me and touching yourself at the same time."

He shot Vorx an annoyed look before addressing me again.

"Solin watches Brooke sleep while he strokes his cock. If she wakes up before he finishes, she will offer to use her hands or mouth if she is too sore to let him sink his—"

"Stop! What is with you guys? Boundaries. Please. I don't want to hear about other people's sex lives or your plans to touch yourself. I've had one hell of a day and just want to get some sleep."

Turik grunted and picked up his pace.

Ducking deeper into my jacket, I hurried along with them. All I wanted was a bed, a pillow, and a whole heck of a lot of undisturbed silence. Which may or may not happen now. I glanced between Vorx and Turik and reminded myself that the fey respected boundaries. Neither would touch me without permission. And even though Vorx was still smirking at Turik almost as if he was silently goading Turik on, I felt like he would step in and tell Turik to knock it off now that I've said I wouldn't like it. Maybe.

Either way, sleeping in a house not filled with people was a novelty I wanted to embrace. Two fey roommates were plenty. Two felt extra safe without being overwhelming. And I really liked the sound of that.

The house once again struck me as magazine-worthy when I entered, and I struggled to believe I would be able to call this place home on a permanent basis. The house Nat and I had lived in before the earthquakes had been nice enough if a little small. This place, though, was a spacious, well-decorated luxury in comparison.

I stripped out of my jacket and boots, letting the comfortable warmth wrap around me. It was enough heat that I wouldn't need to sleep fully dressed for the first time in a very long time.

That thought collided with the recollection that I'd agreed to sleep in Turik's bed with him...before he told me he planned to stare at me all night while he masturbated.

My gaze drifted to the couch, which looked comfortable enough, then to Turik, who was watching me far too closely.

"What are the chances of me sleeping on the couch without you staring at me throughout the night?" I asked.

"Not good," Vorx answered before Turik could.

"That's what I figured. I don't suppose I could sleep by myself tonight? A lot of things have changed in the last twenty-four hours, and I'd like some time to adjust to it all."

Turik didn't hide his disappointment, but he didn't seem mad either when he agreed to sleep on the couch.

"Thank you. Could I borrow a shirt to sleep in while I wash what I'm wearing? And maybe use the shower?"

"This is your home, too. You don't need to ask to use anything," Turik said. "I'll show you where my shirts are."

He led the way to the master bedroom and opened a drawer full of clean t-shirts.

"Everything I have is yours," he said, gesturing. "And I will not watch you sleep tonight. I promise. But if you wake up and are afraid, promise you will call for me. I want you to know you are safe here."

The sincerity in his gaze set my chest tightening with gratitude.

"Thank you, Turik. I will. I promise."

He grunted and headed for the door. As soon as I knew I was alone, I closed myself in the bathroom, more than ready to wash away the reminders of my past life.

However, some things wouldn't wash away.

The filth of not bathing for several days did, but not the

bruises. The ones that decorated my stomach with vivid yellows and purples and more muted browns were the most recent. A few older ones trailed my hips and upper thighs, and a couple more lightly discolored my ribs. Small ones dotted my breasts—fingermarks from Nat's punishing grip.

There was no washing away my past with him.

I turned off the water and looked down at myself, feeling overwhelming defeat. The bruises would fade with time, but would the fear? I doubted it. Nat had to be awake by now. Would he remember what happened? Would he know where to look for me? I tried to tell myself I was in a house hidden among countless other houses, but it didn't help.

I'd tried running when we'd first gotten married. A friend of a friend had a place out in the middle of nowhere. Nat had found me, and no one had heard my begging and sobbing for the days that followed. I hadn't tried leaving since then.

Lost in thought, I opened the glass shower door and reached for the towel on the counter. Before I touched it, a noise sounded to my right like a mix of a pained hiss and a growl. I turned my head so fast that hair lashed my face. But it didn't prevent me from seeing Turik.

He stood in front of the linen closet just inside the door. The blanket he held fell to the floor as he took a step in my direction. My gaze flew to his. Anger unlike anything I'd ever witnessed darkened his expression.

Panic squeezed the air from my lungs, and I retreated a step.

Another low growl filled the room as he slowly prowled forward.

Desperate, I grabbed the shower door and shut it, even though I knew the meager barrier would do nothing to slow him. Pressed back against the wet tiles, I watched him stop in front of the glass.

His gaze wasn't locked with mine but swept over me from breast to thighs. Slowly, he lifted his gaze and set a palm on the glass.

"Mya says that we cannot kill humans. That every life matters because there are so few humans left. But I will tell Drav and my brothers what I've seen, Shelby. The male who did this to you? His life will no longer matter. I promise you that."

A shiver ran through me at the menace behind those words and at the very real hope I felt that he meant them.

Turik took a step back and opened the glass door. However, he didn't come into the shower. He simply offered his hand.

"I know you need time to adjust and want to sleep alone tonight. You will have both. But will you let me help you? I want you to feel safe. Maybe for the first time in a long time?"

I studied his muscled bulk and large hands that I knew could rip a head clean off. Then, his pointed ears, reptilian eyes, and smooth grey skin. He wasn't Nat. Turik and his brothers would never lift a hand against a woman. They truly cherished each one of us.

And they desperately wanted to be needed in return.

A shaky sigh escaped me, and I left the wall to place my hand in his.

"I'd really like that," I said.

He grunted and reached for my towel as he helped me out of the shower. A second later, the fluffy material enveloped me, and his big hands gently rubbed over my arms and back.

I'd thought he'd simply meant a helping hand so I wouldn't slip, not that he intended to dry me off like a toddler. It should have felt weird, but it didn't. He was so gentle, especially around my bruised middle. I felt coddled and cherished.

"Are you too tired to see Cassie?" he asked when he finished. "She should look at your bruises."

I'd never met Cassie, Tolerance's acting nurse-slash-doctor, and preferred to keep it that way. Too many questions and the resulting pity was the last thing I needed from anyone.

"I'm fine, Turik. They'll fade on their own."

He grunted and opened a drawer that held a selection of hairbrushes while I tugged his clean shirt over my head.

"Do they hurt?" he asked.

They did, but I wasn't going to tell him that. He would insist on visiting Cassie then, and I only wanted sleep.

"I just want to snuggle into that bed and sleep through the whole night without anyone creeping in here and bothering me. I'm sure some of these marks will be gone by morning."

He considered me for a long moment then opened the bathroom door.

"Come. I will brush your hair for you. But if the bruises hurt, you will tell me even if you are tired. I can carry you to Cassie."

His firm authority on the matter made me smile as he strode into the bedroom. Having someone care felt pretty good. Having someone take care of me? Well, that was damn near euphoric and addictive. I wanted more.

Turik sat in the center of the bed and leaned back against the headboard a moment before he patted the area between his spread legs.

The position flexed his abs, and without his shirt to block the view, I couldn't *not* see them. Or the girth of his massive, chiseled thighs. Or his corded throat. Why was I looking at his throat? Shit. Why was I noticing any of it?

Realizing I was just standing there staring at him, I jerked my gaze to his and blamed his stupid masturbation comment on it all.

"I won't hurt you, Shelby. You are safe with me."

CHAPTER EIGHT

I HESITATED A MOMENT BEFORE CAREFULLY SCOOTING MYSELF ONTO the bed. It was a little breezy under the shirt since it only fell to mid-thigh—a reminder of the laundry I needed to do so I would have underwear the next day.

My side brushed against his thigh as I primly sat between his legs.

"Sorry," I said, straightening away.

"You can touch me. I don't mind."

Considering what he'd planned to do while I slept, I was sure he wouldn't mind. The small smile tugging at my lips vanished at the first gentle pull of the brush through my hair.

I almost moaned out loud.

"Is this good?" he asked.

"So good."

I told myself I'd have time to wash my clothes after he was done and settled in for some pampering. He worked through the tangles with the patience of a saint and the lightest of touches, running his fingers over my hair almost like he was petting me. I didn't mind in the least. Each touch was soothing heaven.

My rigid position began to wilt, and I didn't notice how much until my side touched his leg again.

"Sorry," I murmured.

"No apologies are necessary. Relax, Shelby. You are safe with me."

He was right. I was safe. Exhaling more of my tension, I leaned against his right leg, looping an arm around it so I could rest my cheek on his knee while he worked.

My lids started to droop. Between the light stroke of the brush, the heat coming from his leg, and my full belly, the day's tensions melted away, and I closed my eyes in pleasure and exhaustion.

"WHAT IF SHE turns her head and my cock accidentally slips into her mouth? If I don't move, then I am still not touching her. She is touching me, and I consent."

"Your cock will not slip into her mouth. Her mouth is too small. But, yes, you would not be touching her without consent. She would be touching you."

The conversation penetrated my sleep-fogged brain and confused the hell out of me. As did the weird pulsing under my cheek.

"It is going to take many washings to get all of that out of her hair. She will not be happy," Vorx said ominously.

"She kept rubbing her cheek against me. I could not help my reaction. Tell me again what her pussy looks like. I wish I could see it from here."

My eyes popped open, and I sat up fast. Or at least, I tried to. A tug on my hair sent me sprawling face first between Turik's legs. The thing that had felt like an arm, but which was actually his massive erection, met my nose and lips with bruising force. He grunted and hissed out a breath. I groaned and pressed my hands against his thighs for leverage, even as his package twitched against my face.

Lifting my head, I focused on what had my hair. It wasn't his hands. Those were fisted at his sides. No, my hair was plastered to his washboard abs, glued there by cum from the swollen, purple-grey head peeking above the line of his pants.

"You're breathing on it," Turik rasped.

The appendage in question twitched twice, growing darker in color.

Frantically, I gathered my hair in one hand and tugged it free before he made matters worse.

"It's open now," Vorx said from behind me. "It's pink like the tongue of a cow, and the hair around it is short."

My eyes bulged, and I jerked upright from my all-fours position as Turik groaned and cupped himself.

"What the hell?" I demanded, visibly shaking. I shot them both panicked glares, but my gaze settled on Turik. "You said I was safe. You said you wouldn't touch me or stare at me. I thought I could trust you." I swiveled to Vorx. "You had no right to look. You knew you didn't have my consent."

"Forgive me, Shelby," Turik said, calling my attention. "You fell asleep on me before I finished brushing your hair. I knew you were tired and would wake if I tried to leave, so I didn't move. I liked the way you hugged my leg. Then, after a while, you moved your head." His hips twitched. "I tried not to think of how it felt. But you rubbed your face against my cock. I didn't mean to release. I thought it would wake you, but it didn't. I didn't know what to do, so I called for Vorx."

He stopped there, and I could imagine how the rest played out. My cooter had likely been exposed to Vorx the moment he walked into the room.

Scowling, I carefully scooted off the bed.

"I'm going to go wash all of this out of my hair. Please be out of this room by the time I'm done."

After shutting myself in the bathroom, I braced my hands on the counter and gave myself a minute to calm down while the water warmed. When I lifted my head and caught sight of my reflection in the mirror, I cringed.

A mass of tangled hair about the size of a dinner plate stuck out from the side of my head. I gingerly touched the sticky web. He'd saturated it. How was there so much? How many times had he come?

I frowned at myself. Had I escaped one manipulative, controlling monster only to end up with another one? Turik knew damn well I wasn't interested in anything sexual. That I'd only wanted undisturbed sleep. What happened to consent? How could he ignore everything that I'd told him?

Probably because, for the first time in his life, he'd experienced a woman cuddled up to him and would have rather chewed off his own arm than give up the experience, a little voice inside of me whispered.

Hadn't he admitted as much?

The frown disappeared from my face as I tried putting myself in his shoes.

Turik hadn't actually done anything wrong. I'd fallen asleep on him. His choice not to wake me had been made in consideration for me. How was he supposed to know that I'd nuzzle his groin in my sleep and he'd explode all over my hair?

Vorx, however, was another story. He'd definitely gone against everything I'd asked of them when he'd stared at me while I slept. I still had a right to be mad about that. Yet, that little voice whispered to me again.

Of course, he'd stared. Hadn't I stared long and hard when the fey first arrived at Whiteman Air Force Base?

Feeling a bit of guilt for my part in the whole mess, I removed my shirt with care so I wouldn't get it dirty and got into the shower. I'd only just closed the door when I heard someone enter the bathroom.

"I get that the fey lack personal boundaries, but we humans usually shower—"

I forgot how to speak when completely naked Turik stepped into view, looking very remorseful. Not that my gaze lingered on his face. No, it went straight to his massive erection. The very one that had felt like an arm beneath my cheek.

Dear heaven above, I didn't know they came in that size. How is he still hard?

"This might help," he said, holding out a bottle of something.

My mouth opened, and I attempted to form words but didn't manage any sounds. My focus remained locked on that bobbing appendage as he moved closer and opened the shower door. His cock had a slight curve to it, so its head almost tapped his washboard abs...above his belly button.

My insides went hot and cold, and I shuffled back a step when he entered.

"Will you let me wash it out of your hair? I understand now that I should have moved even if it woke you."

The fingers of his free hand captured my chin and forced my gaze up to meet his.

"I am very sorry, Shelby. Truly. Please give me a chance to make amends."

The sincerity in his eyes broke through my shock and won my forgiveness.

"It's okay. I understand," I said. "You weren't trying to manipulate the situation. You were trying to help me. There's no need for a co-ed shower. But—" I gingerly lifted the tangled web of hair that I hadn't wet yet. "You do understand that this would make any woman pretty mad, no matter how it happened, right?"

"I do. And I can see how much you don't like touching it. Let me wash it for you. Let me fix my mistake."

"Are you sure this is about fixing the mess you made?"

My gaze dipped to his erection, but didn't linger there long enough to miss the flicker of raw need that crept into his expression before it quickly disappeared.

"Yes. Right now, I only want to wash your hair and show you that I can keep my word."

Despite how I'd woken, I'd slept better than I had in a long time. Undisturbed and safe. Because of him. Because he'd held me all night long, disregarding his own comfort for mine. When was the last time someone put my needs first? And how stupid was I to want more of that regardless of the trouble it had already caused?

"Okay."

He closed the gap between us, and I blinked at the up-close view of his chest inches from my face. The corded muscles undulated as he reached up and guided my head back. His fingers oh-so-gently smoothed over my hair as he wet it.

Like the night before, he was infinitely gentle and didn't rush the process. This time, however, he studied my face as he massaged my scalp and worked through the tangles. And I saw every flicker of desire that crossed his expression.

Unable to handle the scrutiny or how hard he was trying not to let his want show, I closed my eyes. It didn't stop what he was feeling, though, which he wasn't afraid to share with words.

"You are so beautiful, Shelby. I ache for a female of my own when I watch you. You are soft and so different from me. I know I've made many mistakes in a short time, but I swear I am learning how to be a better man for you."

His words melted what little anger remained, and I opened my eyes to look up at him.

"You started out as a better man, Turik. I'm just not ready for another one. I want to be by myself for a while."

"You want to live alone?"

"No. I don't mind sharing a house. In fact, it helps me feel safer knowing both you and Vorx are here. I just meant that I want to be single. Being with Nat wasn't good, and I need some time to let that fade."

Turik released my hair and pulled back to look at my torso.

"Like your bruises."

"Exactly."

He exhaled heavily and nodded.

"I understand."

"Thank you. I think I can handle my hair from here."

He didn't try to wheedle more time or touch me in any way. He simply left, and I stared at his backside the whole time.

Why did the fey have to be so temptingly sculpted? I lightly bit my lip then focused on washing my hair a second time. He'd done well, though, and there wasn't a trace of him left.

When I emerged from the shower, the sky was already brightening with the light of a new day, and my clothes waited for me, folded, on the counter. They didn't just look clean; they smelled clean too. I lifted the socks to my nose and gave a tentative sniff, inhaling the light scent of detergent.

Since Turik had been pinned under me all night, I knew my clean clothes were Vorx's doing. It almost made up for the line he crossed this morning.

Almost.

If he was as smooth as Turik with his words, I would probably be over my grudge by nightfall.

Dressed in clean clothes and fully covered, I left the bathroom and joined my housemates in the kitchen. Turik was already dressed for the day and looking at the contents of the cupboards.

"Which do you prefer?" he asked. "Pancakes, oatmeal, cereal with milk, or eggs?"

"You have all of that?" I asked in disbelief.

"Yes. But if there is something else you want, we can probably find it in the storage shed."

"No. That's okay. Cereal with milk sounds great." I didn't even care what kind of cereal it was. How long had it been since I had such a normal breakfast or tasted milk? Over four months now? Without a way to track the passing days, time had a way of slipping by.

Turik and Vorx worked in unison to prepare my breakfast. Vorx produced a glass filled with milk from the fridge while Turik set out a bowl and spoon for me. The cupboard above the fridge held seven different cereal boxes for me to choose from.

The sugary mix I selected wasn't something I would have normally eaten, but it brought me back to my childhood and happy memories.

I grinned as I shoveled it in, barely noting the way they watched me.

Their attention didn't feel weird. It felt right.

CHAPTER NINE

As soon as I finished my last bite of breakfast, Turik held out his hand.

"We should hurry. Ryan will be waiting."

I glanced from his hand to my bowl. "I'll just clean this—"

Vorx swiped up the dishes and placed them in the sink.

"We will clean when we return," he said.

"Okay."

The moment the word was out of my mouth, I was up in Turik's arms.

"I don't have my shoes on yet."

He paused. Instead of releasing me, his hold fractionally tightened as he glanced toward the entry where my shoes waited. I could almost read the debate going on in his head by the subtle changes in his expression.

"You're considering not letting me down, aren't you?" I asked.

Turik's gaze locked with mine.

"I will never want to let you go. But I won't place my wants before yours again. Would you like me to put you down?"

"Please. I want to walk on my own as much as possible. And I appreciate your honesty. Thank you for that."

The disappointment in his eyes sent a blade of guilt through me. But I didn't take my words back or linger at his side once I gained my footing. I'd been clear. I wasn't in Tolerance to hook up with a fey no matter how badly Turik might want that.

It didn't matter that I knew he would never treat me like Nat had. I needed time to shake off the remnants of that life. And probably even more time to make sure that Nat wouldn't track me down and hurt the people close to me. Turik was already growing on me, and I didn't want anything to happen to him. Vorx either, despite his blatant disregard for personal boundaries.

When we finally emerged from the house, the cloud of my exhale swirled in the crisp predawn air. I didn't mind the cold and inhaled deeply, breathing in the new day.

Shaking away thoughts of Nat and the rough start to the morning, I focused on the homes around us, committing the details to memory. Homes loosely clustered together. Modest yards large enough to support gardens come spring. Houses still small enough to heat with wood stoves and solar panels.

"Good morning!" Ryan called when we neared the wall.

There was another woman with him, and I gave a tentative smile in greeting.

"This is Eden. She volunteered to take another group of fey to check out a few of the areas we circled."

I said a quiet hello and accepted the map that Ryan handed me.

"I divided up the locations between the three of us. Check what you can, but watch your time. If we're not back before dark, Mya will send out fey search parties and no one wants that."

"If you see any humans out there, don't assume they're friendly," Eden added. "Don't approach them. Just note the location, and Matt or Ryan can go and check it out."

"Steer clear of the exiles, too," I said. "They were holed up in an apartment building close to Tenacity."

"No, they are gone from there," Vorx said.

Dread filled my stomach, and I slowly turned my head to look at him.

"What do you mean?" I asked.

"They packed their things and left. All the tents and supplies are gone."

"How do you know?"

"I looked for them last night," Vorx said.

Fear clawed at my insides, making my hands tremble. I pushed it down and fisted my fingers. It didn't matter. Eden's shrewd gaze caught it all.

"Your ex can't get to you here or out there with the fey. You're safe. Trust me. Trust them." Her gaze shifted to Turik, who stood behind me.

As if he was waiting for that signal, he wrapped his arms around me and tugged my back against his chest. Maybe it was because he'd held me all night or simply the knowledge that he would do whatever he could to keep me safe, but I melted into his hold and breathed a little easier as his presence chased away some of the fear and tension.

"I might be safe enough, but what about everyone else? Nat doesn't care who he hurts. He's already shown that. Don't underestimate him."

Several nearby fey grunted, acknowledging the warning

and reminding me that conversations around any fey were rarely private.

"Don't worry about the people here. They'll spread the word," Ryan said. "And Matt and June already know they need to watch out for him. It'll be fine."

Fine? I fought to swallow my sputter and insane laughter. There was so much about the current state of things that was not fine, and Nat running around loose was one of them.

"Unless there's anything else, we're wasting daylight," I said, not wanting to contradict Ryan further.

He flashed a grin at me.

"No, ma'am." He turned to the fey. "We need three groups of about fifteen to twenty each."

There were a few disappointed groans and movement between nearby houses. It wasn't until then that I realized how many of the fey had gathered.

"Remember, no unnecessary risks," Ryan said just before walking away to join one of the groups gathering by the wall.

Eden turned to the big fey behind her.

"Well, Ghua? Ready for a day of fresh air?"

"I would rather stay and—"

He grinned behind the small hand suddenly covering his mouth, and she shot me an apologetic look before he bent and picked her up.

"Have fun!" she called just before he jumped over the wall with her.

I opened the map and looked down at the locations Ryan had circled, then at the direction of the rising sun to orient myself.

"Ready to go house shopping?" I asked Turik.

He immediately lifted me into his arms.

"Tell us where to go."

THE TURNING LANE leading into the neighborhood held promise. That sign of traffic likely meant we would find more than the handful of clustered homes we could see.

In the hours since our group had left Tolerance, we hadn't found anything remotely like the settlements already established. However, our time hadn't been all uselessly spent. While looking around, I'd marked the map where we'd found homes with wood stoves or solar panels or whatever other supplies anyone would find useful. We'd hit the jackpot in one home when we found a freezer loaded with convenience foods. I'd eaten a whole pizza for lunch—best pizza of my life.

Snapping myself out of my pizza daydream, I scanned the houses at the neighborhood entrance.

"If it extends back several blocks, it could work," I said quietly. "Ready to explore?"

Turik's gaze, which had been on the homes ahead, dropped to mine. Tenderness flitted across his expression, and he shifted my weight slightly. Except for lunch and a bathroom break, he hadn't put me down. And I didn't exactly mind since I knew I was far safer in his arms when outside Tolerance's protective walls.

"We are ready," he answered.

"Let's go to the house with the reddish-brown roof and see what we can spot from up there."

He grunted and took off at a sprint. I tucked my face into his chest and waited for the stomach-roiling jump. It didn't take long. I felt us leave the ground, and a moment later, he landed with a soft thud.

I lifted my head to look around and froze at the sound of the unholy howl that echoed around us. It wasn't the mournful cry of a wolf or the pleading song of a domesticated dog. This was a sound not meant to be heard by human ears. A sound that foretold of death or much worse.

And it was much too close.

The fey on the roof with us looked at the fey still on the ground, and my gaze followed. Not a moment later, infected flooded out of the house beneath us. One of the fey below disappeared under the wash of bodies, buried as they piled over him.

"Turik," I said, pointing to where the lost fey had been.

Another howl rang out, followed by a snarl that had the hair on my arms standing on end. The moans of the infected escalated, and a few fey shouted out a moment before a dark shape bolted into the mass of rotting corpses.

My eyes rounded at the sight of a hellhound in daylight. That wasn't supposed to happen. They avoided light at all costs. I'd been told that it hurt them, which appeared to be true based on the smoke curling from its black, decaying skin.

It spun around to face the house when it reached the front lawn. Its glowing red gaze whipped up to the roof and fixated on me. A long string of saliva dripped from its pulled-back lips.

Before I could comprehend the hound's intentions, it launched itself toward us.

Toward me.

Turik pivoted to place himself between me and the hell demon.

"Stop the hound!" Turik yelled, sprinting across the roof at the same time the nearby fey moved to intercept it.

He jumped, and I looked over his shoulder. Two of the fey followed us while the rest held back the monster. The hound's focus never wavered from me as it thrashed to escape their collective holds.

The melee disappeared from sight as Turik leapt down from the roof. He never paused running when he hit the ground. Infected were everywhere. Two new fey flanked us. An infected rushed at our group, and at the squelching head removal, I pressed my face to Turik's chest to shield myself from the spatter.

"I trust you," I said, holding onto him.

Another howl rang out, followed by a round of vicious snarling that abruptly cut off.

"It's dead!" someone yelled.

Turik jumped again, but as soon as he landed, he stood me on the roof. His fingers pinched my chin and forced my head back. His gaze swept wildly over my face before he began tugging up my sleeves to look at my skin.

Understanding hit me.

"Turik, I'm fine. I wasn't bitten."

Rather than speak, he simply tugged me into his arms and held me close.

"Stay there," another fey called from below. "We will check the rest of the homes."

Turik continued to hold me with his arms locked tightly around my shoulders.

"Hey," I said gently, lifting my hands to his waist. "It's okay."

But it wasn't. My hands landed on too much wetness, and I

didn't need to look to know it was blood. If he was that coated...

I stepped back in his hold and looked down at myself. My upper body, shielded by him, wasn't bad. My shoes and jeans up to mid-calf were a mess, though.

Comprehending the seriousness of the situation, I twisted to look down at the fey.

"Was anyone hurt?" I asked.

"Gyrik and Vorx were, but not as badly as Uan. They will heal," one of the fey said from below.

"Vorx?" I asked in shock.

Turik's arm locked around my waist when I tried moving closer to the edge.

"I am here," a tired voice called. My gaze swept the carnage below until I spotted Vorx sitting on a patch of dead lawn a few houses away. His ripped shirt glistened wetly over his ribs.

I cringed twice over–the first time when I saw the blood and the second time when I saw no one was helping him. Not that I knew how, either. I could slap a Band-Aid on a scrape, and that was about it.

"How bad is it?" I asked.

"I will heal."

Was that the manly answer for "get me to the hospital now?"

I lifted my gaze and surveyed the surrounding homes. From my rooftop position, I could see several offshoots to the main road and rooftops extended beyond the first two sets. Good enough to know there was more to this place.

Turning back to Vorx, I said, "Let's head back and get you and Gyrik looked at by Cassie."

"Are you sure?" Turik asked. "There are more markings on your map."

"Ryan said not to take risks. We now have two wounded fey on top of a very close call. That hellhound shouldn't have come after me in daylight. We need to head back and let the others know."

Turik grunted and scooped me up.

Nestled in his arms, I watched Vorx's effort to stand and acknowledged just how much I owed the fey. If he and the others hadn't stopped the hellhound, I would have been laying among the infected bodies by now.

I tipped my head to look up at Turik's grim face.

I owed them both.

CHAPTER TEN

AFTER WITNESSING GYRIK AND VORX'S STRUGGLES TO GET HOME, I tried not to think about my stinging legs as I knocked on the door in front of me. My discomfort seemed so trivial compared to theirs.

The door swung open, and Ryan's mother took one look at me before ushering us in. Eden and Ghua already stood in the entry. They were dirty but not bloody like Turik and I were.

Aware of my filth, I didn't move any farther into the house after Julie shut the door behind us.

"What happened?" she asked.

"We had a run-in with a hellhound and a large herd of infected," I said. "Vorx and Gyrik were hurt. They're already at Cassie's, getting stitched by Kerr." I looked at Eden. "Did your group run into trouble too?"

"No. Just the opposite. I think we found the perfect place. It's a cluster of at least fifty houses around a large pond with fish. Cattle here. Fish there. It's a match made in heaven. What about you? Did you find anything?"

"The neighborhood where we ran into the hellhound

might be an option. I didn't count the houses, but it looked like a decent number." I handed over the map to Julie. "I crossed out the locations that wouldn't work and marked the one that might. Can you let Ryan know? I want to get back to Vorx."

"Of course. Tell Vorx we're thinking of him, and let us know if you need anything."

I nodded and led the way out of the house.

"He'll be okay, right?" I asked Turik yet again.

"He will be in much pain for several days, but he will heal."

The answer didn't make me feel any better than it had the first time he'd said it.

"If I hadn't been there, that hellhound wouldn't have—"

Turik stopped and turned me toward him.

"No. My brothers and I need to kill every last hound to save the humans who remain. Do you understand? Humans are our hope, Shelby. Each of my brothers will risk himself to protect our futures. Vorx's injuries are not your fault. They are a necessary step in obtaining what he wants most."

Females. Just like every other fey. And that was why they seemed so chill when I warned them about Nat. Not that they weren't taking the threat seriously. They were simply chalking up dealing with him as another necessary step.

I slowly nodded, hating that the fey were risking so much when it felt like I'd risked so little. Sure, leaving Nat hadn't been easy. It continued to terrify me. Yet, the idea of facing a hellhound like they did made the threat of Nat seem laughable in comparison.

We walked the rest of the way to Cassie's in silence and let ourselves in without knocking, as she'd instructed since it was nap time for the kids.

"How's it going?" I asked softly, just inside the door, knowing Kerr would hear.

A minute later, Cassie joined us, her expression pinched.

"It's going," she said. "That mother trucker got him to the bone. Why in the heck didn't someone carry him? He had to be dying in pain."

Guilt dropped like a lead ball in my stomach, and it must have shown on my face because Turik's hands immediately settled on my waist.

"He is stubborn," Turik said. "Maybe next time, he will be less stubborn."

Cassie rolled her eyes at him before focusing on me again.

"You might as well go home and clean up. It's going to take Kerr a while. I'll make sure someone walks Vorx back when he's done. And you all are getting some first aid lessons. You should have known he would make his injuries worse by running the whole way back."

Turik grunted, and she gave him a stern look before walking away while grumbling about stubbornness being a universal trait.

"Maybe you should stay here to help him home," I said. "I can find my own way."

"No. I will stay with you," he said. "My brothers will help Vorx and Gyrik."

The entire walk home, the attack replayed in my head. The injuries the fey received would have been superficial if that stupid beast had only followed the rules. After all, the infected were nothing to the fey—a nuisance at best.

Once we reached the house, I had no choice but to strip down to my shirt and underwear just inside the door. Not that

Turik minded as he took each discarded item from me and promised to wash them so I would have them tomorrow.

I walked away from him, feeling his gaze on my backside. And it wasn't a horrible feeling. In fact, it was a nice distraction from the guilt I carried.

It wasn't until I was in the shower that I realized what I'd overlooked regarding the attack. The infected had been in the house with the hound. Considering how many bodies we'd left behind, they had to have been packed in there.

Why?

Since the day of the earthquakes and the first time Nat spotted an infected, I'd never seen a hellhound and infected together like that. What did it mean?

I opened my mouth to call for Turik before snapping it shut and rinsing my hair. My questions could wait until I had clothes on.

Clean of infected blood, I turned off the water and reached for my towel. The underclothes I'd worn today were already gone, replaced by a neatly folded pile of string and a see-through tee-shirt.

"Oh, hell no," I said softly, picking up the thong.

"Turik," I called. "I am not wearing this."

I wrapped a towel around my torso and opened the bathroom door. Sure enough, the fey in question waited there. But his expression wasn't one of eager anticipation. Worry pulled at his features, and a clean white tee dangled from his hand.

"Azio gave those clothes to Terri. They frightened her because she thought they were sex clothes. They weren't. Azio only wanted to see her breasts to help her."

"How in the hell would seeing her breasts help her?" I asked.

"Ghua told Azio that Eden's nipples get darker just before her period. That's when her breasts ache and need gentle massages. Azio only wanted to watch for signs of pain. But that's not why I'm hoping you'll wear those clothes."

I waited for him to connect the dots for me, but he didn't.

"Okay. I give up," I said when he paused for too long. "Why do you want me to wear them if it's not for sex or boob pain? And it better be a very good reason after the way I woke up this morning."

"Groth lives with Azio and Terri. He forgets things when Terri wears the shirts. They are distracting. Maybe Vorx will forget his pain and you will forget your guilt?"

He handed me the oversized white tee-shirt, and stunned by his insight, I robotically accepted it.

"It is your choice, Shelby."

I realized the clothing choice wasn't just about Vorx and me.

"You're worried about him, too, aren't you?"

Turik studied me for a long moment.

"This isn't Vorx's first hellhound injury. We both carry scars from them. Yes, he is hurt badly and in pain, but I know he will heal. I am more worried that your feelings of self-blame will drive you to want to leave. That is what Vorx and I fear most."

With that, he walked away.

I slowly shut the bathroom door and looked at my clothing options. Wear the see-through shirt and thong or a nice, white t-shirt that would cover me? Two minutes ago, the choice was simple. Now, not so much.

What Turik had said ran through my head. If Vorx was really in that much pain, would dressing in the "sex clothes," as

Turik put it, really distract him from it? I highly doubted it. But it would show them both then I was invested in staying here. That I was trying to purge my guilt over what had happened.

I rolled my eyes and gave myself a hard look.

"Call it what it is, Shelby," I whispered.

Yes, I owed Turik and Vorx for their efforts in keeping me safe. Knocking out Nat and his men, giving me a place to stay, and protecting me from the infected and hellhound absolutely indebted me to them. But not enough that I'd feel the need to parade around them naked out of some sense of obligation.

Unless I wanted to do it.

A flush brightened my face as I folded the white shirt and picked up the thong. I didn't possess an ounce of body shame. There was no point in it. Tits were tits. Legs were legs. And an ass was an ass. It didn't matter what shape they came in. Men liked them small and firm or large and slightly saggy. The right man would want me just the way I was. I'd known that long before I ever met Nat.

And because of Nat, this also wouldn't be the first time I wore skimpy clothes around men. Although, this time, it was my choice.

Both the thong and top fit me well enough. However, the thin yellow material "covering" my breasts did little to hide any detail. My nipples were clearly visible, as were the bruises decorating my torso. At least the color of the shirt camouflaged the fading ones on my breasts.

Wearing this wouldn't likely be the type of distraction Turik was hoping for.

I was still frowning at the mirror when I heard voices downstairs. Opening the door, I listened to Turik.

"I will help him to his bed. Thank you, Kerr."

The outer door shut as I made my way to the living room. Both Vorx and Turik stopped their joint progress across the space to stare at me, but I barely registered their shocked and awe-filled gazes. Mine locked on the web of stitches covering Vorx's right side and the large square of gauze covering his outer left thigh.

He leaned on Turik with his left arm around Turik's shoulder for support.

"Does it hurt?" I asked, hurrying to his other side to help. Not that I tried lifting that arm since that was the side with the stitches over his ribs.

"I was about to ask you the same thing," he said, lifting his gaze from my breasts to my eyes.

"I promise your pain is far greater than any discomfort I feel. Is there anything I can do to help? Do you want me to turn down the covers for you?"

"Yes."

I started to hurry away.

"Wait," he called.

Glancing over my shoulder, I caught them both staring at my ass. Their ears were dark grey, and there might have been a twitch in Vorx's athletic shorts when he rasped, "Slower."

Swallowing a snort, I rolled my eyes at him then looked at Turik. His gaze was just as full of hunger.

"Looks like you were right," I said.

"I'm always right."

Vorx laughed then grunted. I knew it was in pain, but nothing else in his body language hinted at it.

"Vorx needs rest and something to eat," Turik said. "Perhaps you can stay with him while I make dinner."

I nodded and continued to Vorx's room, pulling back the

covers so Turik could help settle Vorx in bed. Vorx winced often, but his gaze kept returning to me where I stood on the other side of his bed, and he never complained. As soon as Vorx was settled, Turik left.

"Do you want another pillow behind you so you're sitting up more, or would you rather sleep for a bit?"

"Neither."

"You really should try to sleep. The body heals with sleep."

He grunted and continued to watch me, looking far too alert.

"What if I brush your hair for you? That put me right to sleep last night."

"Yes. My brush is over there." He glanced at a dresser and watched me cross the room to fetch it.

"Where can I sit that won't hurt you?"

His lips curved slightly.

"You can sit anywhere. You won't hurt me."

This time I snorted.

"I'm tempted to sit on your chest and prove otherwise."

His eyes changed from one heartbeat to the next. His vertically slitted pupils ballooned to circles, nearly obliterating his pale green irises.

"Sitting on my chest would cause discomfort but more pleasure than pain." He moved his arms away from his sides. "Come try it."

CHAPTER ELEVEN

I SHOOK MY HEAD AT VORX AND HIS RIDICULOUS SUGGESTION TO SIT on him.

"When Turik said this—" I gestured at myself, "—would distract you, I didn't believe him. But all you fey only have one thing on your minds, don't you?"

The moment I leaned forward to join him on the bed, his gaze dropped to my breasts. My B cups didn't move a lot in general, but apparently, dangle mode was an over-the-top awesome way to display them. And after the months of abuse I'd endured, the appreciative way Vorx simply watched me was a balm to my soul.

As soon as I settled near his head, I picked up a length of his still-damp hair and started brushing. While the room slowly filled with the scent of dinner, Vorx's pupils returned to their normal size, and his eyelids began to droop. I kept it up until my arms grew tired and his eyes finally closed.

Smiling slightly, I leaned in and gently kissed his forehead.

When I straightened, I glimpsed Turik in the doorway and lifted my fingers to my lips to indicate he should be quiet. He didn't say anything as I carefully eased off the bed and returned the brush to Vorx's dresser, but there was definite heat in Turik's gaze when I joined him in the hallway and mostly closed Vorx's door.

Again, I didn't mind the look. No, I basked in it.

"Maybe we should keep his dinner warm and let him sleep for a while," I said softly.

Turik grunted and led the way to the kitchen.

"How are you?" I asked. "Anything hurting after all that running and carrying?"

"No. I have no pain."

Yet, even as he said that, he rubbed his hand over his chest like he did.

"Are you sure?"

Instead of answering, he gestured to the plates that waited on the kitchen island. Only two. He must have known Vorx would want to sleep first.

"Do you want to eat here or in the living room?" I asked. "We could watch a movie if you're not tired."

It was still early, and since I hadn't been the one to do all the running, I wasn't ready to turn in yet. I also wanted to stay close enough to Vorx to hear if he woke up and needed anything.

"We can do whatever you'd like. I'm not tired."

I flashed Turik a smile and took both plates.

"Come on, then. Let's check out your movie selection."

After encouraging Turik to sit on the couch, I left the plates on the coffee table and went to inspect his stack of movies. I was very aware of the view I presented when I bent forward and grinned when I heard him shift on the couch behind me.

"I'm glad you had the forethought to close the curtains," I

commented as I browsed. "I'm not exceptionally shy about my body, but I'm not really into public exhibition either. Especially with all my bruises."

"I like your body. I don't like the bruises."

Glancing over my shoulder, I gave him a quick, reassuring smile. "Me either. I'm going to be really glad when they fade." The smile diminished, and I straightened with a random movie in my hand. "Did anything happen here today while we were gone? I should have asked Julie that before we left."

Turik stood and closed the distance between us. When he reached me, he smoothed his hands over my arms. There was no mistaking the tender look in his eyes or that he was trying to comfort me with the gesture.

"You are safe here. Nat no longer deserves any of your thoughts. Give your worry to Vorx."

I felt a tug on my heartstrings and wasn't exactly sure why. Was it because I was so starved for gentle touches and kind words, or because Turik was so open about his concern for people other than himself?

"And you too, right? You still deserve my worry?"

His ears darkened, and his pupils grew just a little larger as his gaze dipped to my chest. Then he shrugged slightly and returned his gaze to my face.

"Only you can decide who is deserving of your worry. Except for Nat. He is no longer deserving."

My smile returned.

"Understood. But my worry was more for the people here than Nat."

He grunted and slid his hands the length of my arms.

"Are you cold?"

My smile widened.

"Is this where you offer to keep me warm?"

"Yes, I can add wood to the stove."

I chuckled and shook my head, loving that the fey, while very interested in attaining a female of their own, didn't stoop to games.

"I'm actually fine. It's comfortable in here. Ready to watch this?" I looked down at the movie in my hand. It was an old classic about a bunch of misfits going on an adventure and finding treasure.

"I am ready."

He took the movie from me and started it while I settled on the couch with my plate. Was this the third meal now that I hadn't needed to cook for myself? Feeling decidedly spoiled, I took my first bite. The chicken breast was seasoned to perfection, and I groaned when I tried the baby potatoes and carrots.

"You have no idea how good it is to eat a vegetable that isn't cooked to nothing and swimming in a thin stew. This is delicious."

"I'm glad you like it. Emily and Mary have been teaching some of us to cook using human spices. Mary said that food was the way to a man's heart, but she thinks it will work the other way around now since food is scarcer."

"She's right about that," I said. "You saw the women lining up for the soup kitchen. Feed them, and you'll win them in no time."

He grunted and started eating his meal as the opening credits rolled.

Once my food was gone, the movie sucked me in, and it wasn't until nearly the end that I heard a pained sound coming from Vorx's room and returned to reality. One where I was comfortably snuggled against Turik's side, and he had an arm casually draped over my shoulder.

"I'll go check on him," I said. "Maybe you can warm up his dinner again?"

Turik's only answer was to lift his arm. I hurried from his side, worried about Vorx, which proved valid when I caught him in the middle of trying to sit up.

"Wait," I said, rushing forward. "Let me help you before you bust a stitch."

He paused what he was doing to look up at me. Or rather, my boobs.

"What are you trying to do? Get more comfortable or get out of bed?" I asked when he said nothing.

"Out of bed. But I changed my mind."

"You hurt yourself, didn't you?" I leaned around him to inspect the stitches along his side.

The hand of his good arm lightly settled on my hip.

"Females are so soft," he murmured with reverence.

"Careful what you say. Some females might take that as an insinuation that they're fat."

"I like all females. Round ones are hard to find, though. Shax is lucky to have Angel."

"Angel? Isn't she the pregnant one close to giving birth?"

"Yes."

I laughed lightly and straightened.

"The stitches look good, but you shouldn't try moving around without help. And Angel's not fat. She's pregnant. There's a difference. If you want a girl with a lot of soft, tempting curves, she needs to be fed more than two lean meals a day. Food is fuel. When we don't burn the fuel, we store it." I patted my hip above his hand. "Usually goes right here for me."

His gaze dipped to where his touch lingered, and he surprised me by sliding his fingers along my skin.

"It is much softer here."

I shook my head. "Thanks, I think. Are you hungry? Turik went to warm your dinner."

"I will eat. Will you stay and talk to me?"

It was only because he was watching my face and not my body that I sat on the end of the bed.

"What would you like to talk about?"

"I want to know more about why you have those bruises. I want to understand why a man would do such a thing. Why did you not come here sooner?"

I knew he didn't understand that those questions caused as much hurt as Nat's fist. Just as I doubted he would understand the reasons I'd stayed. I felt unjudged by his patient stare and tried to shake off the shame and pain threatening to blanket me.

"It's hard to explain. Fear kept me in the end. Fear that, if I tried leaving and he caught me, everything I'd suffered before that would be nothing compared to what he would do to me. It's still there. That fear. Even though you and Turik both say that I'm safe here, I wonder how long it will take Nat to figure out where I am and come for me. What he will do..." I shook my head to dislodge the darker thoughts.

"It was easier to try to appease him," I added. "Safer."

I saw then that was how we'd gotten to the point we had. The cycle of anger and appeasement had slowly escalated over the months. At first, only an apology had been necessary. But Nat's anger had gradually grown. I could still remember the first time he'd grabbed me by the throat and the way I'd excused that behavior in my head.

"You live in fear," Vorx said, his tone deeply troubled.

"Doesn't everyone these days?" I asked with a slight shrug. "We have infected trying to get us. Hellhounds walking around in daylight. Shortages in food. Sure, we're surviving for now, but what happens next when all the pre-existing food goes bad in three to five years? When the solar panels break and there are no replacement parts?"

"We have food animals," Vorx said. "And when the ground thaws, we will plant things."

"There's not enough land inside these walls to feed the animals and humans. We need space outside these walls to grow things. And the infected will be right there waiting for us."

I let out a breath and realized why I'd finally walked away from Nat, even though I knew in my gut that he would come after me and try to hurt people here. Because it didn't matter. Today, tomorrow, in a few months? Deep down, I believed humanity's time was running out.

Troubled, I hugged my knees to my chest and stared at the blanket. When had I so thoroughly given up hope?

Vorx's growling stomach pulled me out of my thoughts, and I looked up to find him studying me.

"I'll go check on your food. Stay put. I mean it."

He grunted, and I felt his lingering gaze on my backside as I walked away.

In the kitchen, I found Turik with a loaded plate.

"Vorx is ready for something to eat, and I think I'm going to turn in early. Any chance you'd be willing to sleep in his room tonight to keep an eye on him? He was trying to stand on his own when he should have asked for help." I hesitated a moment. "And honestly, I'd rather not have a repeat of last night."

"I will sleep with Vorx."

I fought not to smirk at how that sounded.

"Thanks, Turik. I'll see you in the morning."

I waved as I walked away, ready for a little alone time. However, the bedroom didn't feel comfortingly quiet. It felt empty. Scarily so when my thoughts turned to Vorx's questions and Nat.

Rather than sleeping peacefully, I tossed and turned. Minutes stretched to hours until I finally gave up and acknowledged that I didn't feel safe alone.

The house was dark and quiet as I made my way to Vorx's room. Both fey lay in the bed, each on their own side and their feet hanging off the end. The quiet picture immediately wrapped me in a sense of calm, and my gaze settled on the gap between the pair.

I knew where I wanted to be, and it looked like there was just enough space.

CHAPTER TWELVE

Trying not to disturb either of them, I carefully crept onto the bed and settled into place. The heat coming off of Vorx's damaged side lulled me, and I closed my eyes with a quiet exhale. Just as I was drifting off, I felt him lean in and kiss my forehead like I'd done to him.

Turik moved slightly, and a blanket settled over me.

A soft smile curved my lips, and I gave in to the need for sleep.

When I next woke, sweat coated my back and face, and something hard and heavy pressed between my butt cheeks. Frowning, I blinked my eyes open to an up-close view of the chiseled chest I was using for a pillow. I lifted my head and looked at Vorx.

"Good morning, Shelby," he said softly.

"Morning."

I twisted to look at Turik, who was laying on his side, spooning me.

Because he had to.

I'd somehow managed to wedge more room for myself and was lying at an angle, taking up most of the bed.

"Sorry," I murmured, scooting away from his groin where I was doing the pressing.

"For what?" Turik asked.

"Hogging the bed."

"We liked it."

"I could tell." I smirked at him before glancing at Vorx. "I shouldn't have used you as a pillow. I didn't bump the stitches at all, did I?"

He flashed a considerable number of teeth at me. "I didn't feel any pain."

"I bet." I rubbed my hands over my face. "How about I make breakfast this morning while Turik helps you to the bathroom?"

They both grunted, and I crab crawled from my place in bed.

"Thank you, Shelby," Vorx called when I reached the door.

I paused to look back. "Don't thank me until I make something edible."

"Not for breakfast. For the pretty view of your ass. Your breasts and pussy are nice, but your ass is my favorite part."

My mouth dropped open, and a flush exploded on my face. I quickly fled the room.

"I think asses are like pussies," I heard Turik say when I cleared the door. "We can look at them and think about them, but we shouldn't talk about them."

I hurried away before I laughed. Vorx's compliment, while a bit crude, was given sincerely. And it had been a long time since someone told me I looked nice without there being a hidden meaning behind it.

While Turik helped Vorx, I looked over the breakfast options. We had everything needed to make a healthy serving of biscuits and gravy. With my mouth already watering, I set to work.

I was so focused on the end goal that I didn't hear either of them when they emerged from the bathroom. It wasn't until I slipped the biscuits into the oven and turned around that I saw them leaning against the wall, watching me.

I glanced at the messy island and motioned to the chairs on the other side.

"Sit. I'll clean this up. How are the stitches feeling today?"

"They itch," Vorx said, moving with more grace and less wincing than the day before.

"I heard it doesn't take long for the fey to heal, but I'm kind of amazed you're so much better already. When do the stitches come out?" I asked as I cleaned off the counter.

"In three or four days. Ghua's stitches stayed in for seven, and it was too long."

"Good to know." I moved away to start on the gravy. "What are the plans for today, then?"

"Whatever you want to do," Turik said, sitting beside Vorx.

"I'd like to go back to Tenacity and see if Matt would be willing to let me have my old clothes," I glanced back at Vorx. "If you're okay being on your own for a bit."

"I will be fine," he promised.

"You don't need to go back for clothes," Turik said. "There are plenty in the supply shed here. I can take you."

I hadn't been looking forward to returning to Tenacity but had thought my need for underwear would make it unavoidable. Turik's option sounded much better.

"Are my clothes from yesterday clean?" I asked.

"They are." Turik's gaze flicked to my breasts, and he made no move to get the clothes.

Inwardly amused, I turned away from them to finish our breakfast. Their hesitant first bites turned into hungry shoveling and made all the work worthwhile, especially when Turik insisted on doing the clean-up while Vorx fetched my clothes.

A quick shower and change later, Turik and I were on our way to the storage shed.

"Could we stop by Ryan's to see what he found yesterday?" I asked.

"Yes."

Julie greeted us warmly and asked if we'd eaten.

"Shelby made biscuits and gravy. The meat and gravy were delicious."

"Not the biscuits?" I asked.

Turik blinked at me, saying nothing, and Julie chuckled as she led us farther into the house.

"The fey aren't much for the grain-based foods. Or tomatoes. Or okra."

I gave Turik a disgruntled look. "You should have told me."

He grunted. That was it. Likely, he wouldn't ever complain about what I made.

I thought about Nat and how he would throw a plate of food at the wall because he hadn't liked it. Turik's reaction was the far better one. If I had someone cooking for me on a more permanent basis, I sure wouldn't complain about anything they made, either. I'd want to keep them happily cooking for me. Turik was a smart man.

"Ryan's in the study again, looking at the maps and pulling

out his hair. Why don't you see if you can keep him from premature baldness?"

"I can hear you," Ryan called.

Julie grinned, and Ryan looked up at us when Turik and I entered.

"Just the people I was hoping to talk to today. Can you tell me more about the subdivision you found? I know you ran into infected and a hound and that you thought the place had promise, and that's about it."

"Yeah, that pretty much sums it up." I sat in the chair across from him. "The attack happened so fast that I didn't have the time to count the houses, but the number looked decent enough. Eden's sounded more promising, though, with the pond in the middle."

"I agree, but there has to be a reason those infected were in that house with the hound. Some resource we might have missed."

I frowned in thought. "I hadn't considered that. After having that hound chase after me in daylight and Vorx's injuries, I just wanted to get back here."

"I'm not criticizing," Ryan said. "You made the right choice. There's no point in risking more lives than necessary, which is why I'm debating going back there at all. Is the potential for a resource enough of a reason to warrant the risk? If the infected were there once, would it be unsafe to settle there? It's not as close as Tenacity, but neither is Eden's neighborhood."

His hands crept toward his hair.

"If there is some kind of resource there, it's been there for months and will probably be there in another few months. There's no rush to check it out or stress over it. Did you find any promising sites?" I asked.

"Nothing extensive like this place. A small subdivision here and there. Like you, I noted some houses with solars that we can scavenge, but that's about it."

"It would be smarter to scout out Eden's site first. Before the infected notice our interest and flood that location like they did the one I found."

He nodded and looked down at the maps again.

"You're right. I just can't help but wonder what would make the infected protect a hound like that."

"You think they were protecting it?" Turik asked.

"I do. It's just like the farm where we found June. The infected were inside the barn with it. They'd killed a few of the animals, but not many. Did you see any cows roaming around or find any in the house when you cleared it out?"

"None," Turik said.

"So that leaves one other reason they were in that subdivision," Ryan said somberly.

"More humans?" Turik's expression turned troubled, and he glanced at me. "Females?"

"Exactly," Ryan said. "Well, about people being there, not about their genders. I can't think of any other reason the infected and hound would work together, can you?"

"I must speak with Drav. Stay here, Shelby." With a steely glint in his eyes, Turik looked at Ryan. "Keep her safe."

Turik strode away, leaving Ryan smirking at me.

"You know what that means," Ryan said after the front door closed. "Turik's calling dibs."

"I figured that out yesterday when he told you not to kiss me." I shook my head ruefully. "I've explained to both him and Vorx that I'm not interested in a new man. They hear me, but they aren't really listening."

"According to Mya, she had the same trouble with Drav. Look where that landed her."

"I'm honestly trying not to think about that. Surviving one day at a time is enough. Speaking of surviving, we need to figure out where my ex-husband went."

He studied me for a long moment.

"Okay. What do we do when we find him? He's already been exiled."

I slumped in my chair and exhaled heavily, realizing he was right. While Turik and the rest of the fey might be out for blood because of the way Nat treated me, the humans here did not have the same stance, and if I were being honest with myself, I wasn't sure I wanted blood either. However, I couldn't simply ignore that Nat was out there, likely plotting how to get to me.

"Maybe have someone keep an eye on what he and his group are doing?" I asked finally.

Ryan leaned back and considered me, looking very much like his sister.

"I've seen a lot since this all started," he said. "Especially when things started going to shit in Whiteman. Distrust and hopelessness messed with people's heads. The steps Matt and June took in Tenacity cleared some of that. We need to remove the rest. That starts here. Now.

"If you hold on to the past, it will blind you to the future we're trying to build. Instead of holding on to hope, you'll cling to fear.

"I get that trusting the fey to keep you safe is asking a lot. But I'm doing it anyway. They see hope in women like you. Try to see hope in men like them. It's the only way we're going to have a better tomorrow."

After my introspective discovery the night before, Ryan's words affected me deeply.

"Are you a prodigy motivational speaker or something?"

He grinned at me.

"You've met my mom; I had to hone my persuasive skills young."

Julie snorted from the other room, and I returned Ryan's humor even as I dwelled on what he'd said. He wanted me to do more than accept what Turik had been telling me all along as irrefutable—that I was safe here, with the fey. He wanted me to hold on to hope for a better future.

I desperately wanted to, but my old fears clung to me relentlessly.

Having lived with Nat, I knew what he was capable of. He would try to come for me...if he could. And that was where the fey and Ryan might be right; I was letting distrust and fear of Nat cloud my thinking.

Looking for Nat was dangerous at best. Most likely, he was out there struggling to survive, too busy staying alive to worry about me.

"Okay," I said finally. "How soon are the fey going to want to leave to check the subdivision I found?"

CHAPTER THIRTEEN

Waiting for the group to return wasn't easy. Guilt prodded at me—what if there had been people there? People waiting for a rescue? And instead of looking, we'd run.

"Are you hungry, Shelby?" Turik asked.

I shook my head and glanced at Vorx, who quietly watched me instead of the movie playing. If we hadn't left when we had, would he even be here right now? I didn't know the answer to that any more than I would have been able to choose between two lives.

"I'm fine," I said yet again, curling my legs under me.

The clothes Turik and I picked up from the storage shed were much more comfortable than the thong and see-through shirt, and the collection of underwear and bras in the storage room had been more impressive than a big chain store. Now I not only had plenty of undergarments, but I also had an assortment of leggings, jeans, and sweaters.

Turik caught my big toe between his fingers and gently tugged my leg straight, so my foot rested in his lap. Then he started rubbing.

"You are not fine. You are upset, and we don't understand why. We can't help fix the problem if we don't know what it is."

"You are so sweet, Turik. I'm worried. It seems to be what I do best lately. Worry about everything."

"What are you worried about right now?"

"The fey who went out to check the subdivision. I'm worried someone else will get hurt. I'm worried they'll find people and say that they're dead because we didn't stay and look. I'm worried that I'm going to keep making stupid mistakes that cause problems for other people."

Turik and Vorx grunted almost in unison. After my outpouring, the shared, noncommittal response was too funny not to grin.

"I really like that neither of you are high-strung like me."

"You are not high-strung," Turik said, his fingers methodically melting away my tension.

I shrugged lightly. "I keep a lot inside. It doesn't do any good to show the world what I'm feeling."

"Not the world. Me."

"Me too," Vorx added. "We want you to be happy here."

I sighed and put my other foot in Turik's lap. He immediately started rubbing that one too.

"I *am* happy here, but that doesn't erase the worries. It's like how you enjoy having me here but worry that I'm not happy."

Both men grunted again, this time contemplatively.

"Your distraction helped me forget my worries," Vorx said. "Would you like me to remove my pants?"

I almost barked out a laugh, managing to swallow it down at the last minute.

"Thank you for the offer, but no. I don't think I'm ready for that level of distraction. What else do you do to distract yourselves?"

"Think about females," Turik said immediately.

"And before there were females?"

"We hunted and fished and farmed," Turik said. "And we challenged each other."

"Challenged?"

"Fights to test our strength."

"Ah. Yeah, those might not be the best idea to distract me. I enjoy fishing, though. I used to go with my dad all the time." With the typical bittersweet pang, I thought of my father. "He passed away a few years ago. I loved fishing with him. I wouldn't mind trying that. Do any fey go out to fish?"

"No," Turik said, finding a sweet spot on my foot that nearly made my eyes roll back.

"Do you think we could find a boat?" I asked after a blissful moment.

"Yes. Ryan has already collected a few. They weigh nothing and are easy to carry."

"Maybe tomorrow we can try fishing." I paused, the worry creeping back in for the fey who'd left to search the hellhound neighborhood. "Do you think that they'll stay out there all night?"

After Turik had returned from his meeting with Drav, everything had happened so fast. Drav had called for volunteers to go to the subdivision, and Ryan had left with a group three times the size of mine. They planned to scour that subdivision, top to bottom. If they found nothing, they would immediately go to Eden's subdivision.

"If Eden's location is good, they will start collecting nearby vehicles to wall it in. Don't worry, Shelby. Ryan is safe."

I sighed and tugged my feet from his grasp to shift position. He lifted his arm to give me more room to snuggle against his side.

"I know the fey will keep him safe. Just like I know that you and all your brothers will do everything in your power to keep the rest of us safe. I'll try to stop worrying."

His fingers brushed over my side, tickling the bruises still there.

"Thank you for trusting us, Shelby."

"Thank you for insisting."

He chuckled. The sound was the warmest, best thing I'd heard in a very long time. Grinning, I settled my head against his chest and finally focused on the movie, letting his gentle finger strokes soothe me.

When it was time for bed, I once again retreated to Turik's room while he stayed downstairs with Vorx. Maybe I was too used to sleeping in a house full of people, or maybe I knew where I was safest because, no matter how much I tried to fall asleep alone in that bed, I couldn't.

Sighing, I tossed the covers back and padded softly from my room. The base of Turik's t-shirt brushed my thighs as I moved silently down the hall. There was just enough light shining in through the curtains to see where I was going but not enough once I reached their bedroom to see if they were awake or not.

Like the night before, there was a nice Shelby-size gap between the two of them, and I didn't hesitate to fill the space.

Their heat enveloped me. Content, I closed my eyes and drifted off.

I didn't even question the hard length pressing my backside the next morning. But I did lift my head to check who I was laying on. Turik this time. I cringed and looked back at Vorx.

"You shouldn't be lying on your bad side. Why didn't you shove me over? Or turn the other way?"

"And miss this?" he asked, lightly smoothing a hand over my hip. "Never."

A zing of heat shot through me, which I squashed before rolling my eyes and looking down at Turik.

"You need to protect him from his own stupidity. He probably ripped a stitch."

"I've felt the way you wiggle your curves against my cock and would gladly endure a hellhound's claws to feel it again. A few broken stitches are nothing."

"Not helping," I muttered.

I knew sleeping in the same bed with them wasn't right. I knew I should get up and return to my room. But instead of scooting away, I settled back into place. For once, I was doing something selfish and just for myself. I liked the snuggling too much to leave.

Vorx continued to stroke my hip but didn't grind against me even though I could feel the pulsing throb in his length. Turik pressed a kiss to the top of my head and stroked my hair. My fingers traced over the contours of Turik's chest. Under my cheek, I could hear the faint beat of his heart.

Guilt started to nibble holes in the moment.

"I like this," I said after a few minutes. "These last two nights were the first time in a long time that I was able to sleep peacefully. But sleeping like this isn't fair to either of you. I'm sending mixed signals by saying that I don't want a relationship and then sneaking in here."

"No, you're not," Turik insisted, his arm coming around my shoulders to hug me.

Vorx moved closer, so it wasn't just our hips connecting. His chest heated my back as he hugged me from behind too.

I reveled in the sensation so much I almost didn't hear what he said next.

"You said you need time to heal. You can take all the time you need. We understand why you want this. It is safety."

"And comfort," Turik added. "Our cocks are too simple to understand that. But our minds understand it perfectly."

I burst out laughing and pressed my lips to his chest without thinking. While I froze, he didn't. His hand languidly continued stroking my arm, and Vorx's continued along my hip and side.

Slowly, I exhaled and took the moment for what it was. Safety and comfort from the two men I was growing to trust.

"If we want to go fishing today, we should leave this bed," Turik said after a while. "But I would be happy to spend the whole day like this too."

I smiled against his chest and lifted my head to look down at him.

"Let's go fishing. It'll be a good distraction and a useful way to contribute. We can note any decent fishing holes we find for when the weather turns nice and Ryan wants to stock the new settlement's pond."

Turik grunted and didn't try to stop my withdrawal. Vorx, however, made a low sound that sent goosebumps skittering along my arm when my ass slid across his length.

"Sorry," I murmured before I bolted.

Cheeks still flushed, I cleaned up in Turik's bathroom and dressed for the day. I glimpsed myself in the mirror and saw the oldest bruises had faded to nothing, as I'd predicted. The newest ones were still vivid, but I knew those would eventually fade too. Then what? Would I be ready to choose a fey? To sleep with one of them?

My insides went hot and cold at my conflicted thoughts. I liked all the touching now but wasn't sure I wanted to move past that.

By the time I joined them downstairs, Turik and Vorx both waited by the front door. Turik handed me a biscuit and egg sandwich while Vorx held up my coat.

"You look like you're going to come with us," I said, noting his clothes as I shuffled my breakfast from one hand to the other.

Turik turned me when I had the jacket on and did up the front.

"He is," Turik said. "You feel safer with both of us."

"Not if it's going to hurt him I don't." I turned toward Vorx. "I'd rather you stayed here and rested. Please. I'd feel awful if something else happened to you."

"I would feel the same if something happened to you and I wasn't there to stop it."

I narrowed my eyes at him.

"I'm putting my foot down. No. Stay here."

His lips curved, exposing his wickedly pointed canines. "It's cute that you think I'll listen."

My mouth almost fell open. Instead, I turned to Turik.

"Please talk some sense into him."

Turik shrugged slightly, amusement dancing in his eyes.

"I think Vorx would miss you as much as you would miss him." He gently stroked his thumb over my cheek after fixing my collar. "We will not be alone. I wouldn't risk either of you like that. Trust my brothers and me to keep you both safe."

Disgruntled, I nodded and shot Vorx a warning look.

"No ripped stitches, or I'm sleeping in my own bed tonight."

He merely smirked at me, so I bit into my sandwich and followed Turik out the door.

CHAPTER FOURTEEN

THE FEY HAD A SIZEABLE COLLECTION OF "BOATS," WHICH WERE actually canoes, stacked in someone's backyard. While we inspected each option, word spread quickly that Turik, Vorx, and I were looking to go fishing. Within ten minutes, we had a group of fifteen volunteers with us to carry three of the canoes and a dozen fishing poles.

It didn't take long to reach the first lake south of Warrensburg. A thin sheet of ice clung to the shoreline, not that it deterred the fey from marching through it. Once they'd cleared a decent landing, they launched the canoes, testing them in the open water before returning to the shore.

One had a minor leak, but the other two were fine. While the rest of the fey fished from the shore, the three of us took a canoe to the center. The lake was quiet with only the light breeze and the swish of a cast to keep us company.

We stayed out there until our stringer had three largemouth bass and my face was numb. I could have stayed out there longer, but Vorx caught me shivering and "put his foot down" about returning to shore. Turik, the giant traitor, agreed.

I pretended to pout, but I loved that they were watching out for me.

On shore, the rest of the fey had caught another five fish. I noted the lake on the map that I'd borrowed from Ryan's house and marked the species and the quantity we'd taken.

"Should we try another one?" I asked.

"No," Turik said firmly. He plucked the pencil and map from my grasp, handed both to Vorx, then took my hands and stuffed them down the front of his pants.

The action was so damn unexpected that I immediately tried to jerk my hands out. However, Turik wrapped his arms around me and trapped me against his torso. Immobile, I considered biting.

"Warm them. And your face."

"Are you insane? I could have warmed my hands in my armpits. You just want me touching your eggplant."

"Heh?"

"Your dick." I tried jerking my hands out of his waistband again.

"It's the warmest place. Warmer than anywhere on your body when you're already so cold. The feel of your hands will always bring me pleasure. But in this case, there will also be some pain, which I'm willing to endure, so you are warm."

I tipped my head back and narrowed my eyes at him.

"I'm feeling forced."

"I know." He placed a gentle kiss on my brow. Then another one an inch over. The sting of his warm lips against my skin had me huffing and relenting. Mostly because I knew there wasn't any choice. When it came to my safety, Turik wouldn't give an inch, and his desire to warm me truly was for my safety since I was well past the point of cold.

Feeling like I had a thousand sets of eyes on me instead of sixteen, I pressed the backs of my hands against Turik's groin. He jerked and hissed out a breath—definitely a pained sound.

"Keep going," he encouraged.

There was absolutely something wrong with me. There had to be. Why else would I turn my hands and publicly grope his testicles while grinning into his chest like a madwoman every time he flinched? A few of the other fey chuckled as they packed up the fishing gear.

I knew the moment my hands started to warm, and it had nothing to do with regaining dexterity. The flinching ceased, and Turik's hold on me eased from locked-in-place to gently anchored.

Withdrawing my hands, I stepped away from him.

"I'm not a fan of your technique," I said.

"Next time, I will warm your hands," Vorx said from behind me. "My technique will be much better, and I will flinch less."

I snorted and shook my head at the pair of them.

"Next time, I'm going to keep my hands warm so they don't get shoved where they don't belong."

"Challenge accepted," Turik said. "If Shelby does not stay warm on her own, Vorx can attempt to warm her better. After that, I try again. Best three out of four attempts."

"Wait, what?" I asked.

"Agreed," Vorx said over me, his wolfish grin gleaming.

"I will wager my mattress that Turik warms her best," one of the nearby fey said.

"I will take that wager against a box of chocolate bars," another answered.

"You're all ridiculous," I said, secretly loving their playful banter.

Once the poles were packed and the canoes hefted overhead by the others, Turik picked me up, and our group set out for the next lake. The fey maintained a grueling pace, and the wind lashed my hair and leeched away my warmth. Unsure whether they'd been serious about their bet, I tucked my hands up under Turik's shirt within the first thirty seconds.

He chuckled and pressed another kiss to the top of my head, as if saying, "you're so cute thinking you have a chance." And he wasn't wrong. I truly fought a losing battle this time around since I wasn't starting out fully warm.

By the time we reached the next fishing spot, my legs and backside stung.

Vorx was right there when Turik put me down, and I quickly held up my hands.

"They're warm. See?"

He touched them, and that knowing smirk curved his lips.

"Good. Your hands weren't what I was hoping to warm. Tell me what's cold, Shelby."

"Nothing." My damn body betrayed me with a shiver.

Vorx's grin widened, and behind me, Turik chuckled. Vorx waved to the other fey then pointed to a small cottage at the edge of the water not far from where we stood. Two of them jogged to the structure and disappeared inside.

"Would you like to walk or should I carry you?" Turik asked.

I pouted a bit, crossing my arms as I pretended to think it over. All the while, I held Vorx's gaze.

"How about none of the above? I'm fine. We're here to fish, not to waste time talking."

"We promised to keep you safe, and we will keep our

promise. Even if we have to keep you safe from yourself," Vorx said. "You're too cold to fish. Let me warm you."

"Only if it involves lighting a fire."

He grunted, and a second later, I was up in Turik's arms. I knew better than to believe that grunt was an agreement to a fire.

"I don't think I enjoy being in the center of this challenge. You guys need to find a new game to play."

"We like this one," Turik said. "Back in the caves, Vorx and I always challenged each other. We are evenly matched in physical strength and fighting skills, so we had to find other ways to determine who was the best. Who could bring down the first hound? Who could catch the biggest fish?"

"So everything's a competition?"

"Sometimes," Turik said.

"But not always," Vorx said, glancing back at me. "Sometimes, we work together."

I shivered again and leaned into Turik as we waited for the fey inside the cabin to let us know it was safe. Rather than reemerging through the front door, they came around the side. Blood speckled their chests and faces.

"The house is clear," one called as they both continued toward the lake.

Vorx strode forward and held the door for Turik. Just before he closed the door behind us, I glanced back, saw the fey dive into the water, and shuddered.

"They're going to freeze," I said.

"They will be warmer than you are. I can feel the cold in your legs," Turik said, releasing me. His fingers went to my jacket as he glanced at Vorx. "Her backside is the coldest."

My irritated huff clouded the air.

"Can we light the stove?" I asked, pointing at the cold black potbelly between the very small kitchen and living area at the front of the cabin.

"I will, but it will not warm quickly." He unzipped my jacket and slid it off my shoulders.

Before I could protest, a blanket and a dizzying amount of Vorx enveloped me. With his firm chest pressed against my back and his blanket-supporting arms wrapped around me, I was cocooned in warmth. A few more shivers escaped as I stood there, letting him do his best impersonation of a heated blanket.

"You were right, Vorx," I said after a few minutes. "This is much better than playing with Turik's balls."

Turik snorted.

"I could feel you smile against me. You enjoyed touching me more than you're enjoying standing there."

I scowled at him, but didn't deny it.

"If your back is warm, turn to warm your front," Vorx said, loosening his hold slightly.

I turned in his arms and reached forward, intending to warm my hands on his lower abs, which I knew were far enough from the stitching to be safe to touch. However, I somehow backhanded the massive erection flag-poling between us.

"Where in the hell are your pants?" I asked, jerking my head up to meet his gaze as he grunted from the unintentionally abusive contact.

"Over there," he said, indicating the sofa with a nod. "Your hands are still cold. Touch me again, but more slowly. Your skin needs more time to absorb my heat."

It bounced between us, showing how much he liked the idea of lingering caresses.

"Is that fire lit yet?" I asked, glancing over my shoulder at Turik, who was hunched down on his heels before the stove.

"Yes. But it will take time to make the flames grow. You would warm faster by touching him."

"What happened to choosing me and me having your babies someday?" I demanded without really thinking through what I was saying.

"Nothing," Turik answered calmly. "I still want that."

"You want that and still think I should grope Vorx right now?"

Turik pivoted on his heel to look at me. "This is about keeping you warm, Shelby." He flashed a quick grin at me. "And proving who is better at warming you. I know I will win, so I don't mind."

"You're both annoying," I said, meaning it. I was so annoyed, in fact, that the little devil inside of me found its voice and started to chant, *"Just do it. Do it! Hands on the pole go round and round. Round and round!"*

"Fine," I bit out a moment before I clasped Vorx's length with both hands. Oh, he was hot. So hot. And hard. And long.

His arms banded around my shoulders and pressed me closer to his chest. Not enough to confine my movement, but enough to lean my forehead on his upper abs and watch what I was doing. His cock bobbed and twitched with each stroke, the head turning darker by the second.

A groan echoed through his chest. I grinned and picked up my pace. He bucked into my hands with increasing urgency. I removed one hand and gently squeezed his impressive balls.

Then, I let go.

"All warm," I chirped, patting his hip. "Time to let me go."

I made the mistake of tipping my head back to look up at him.

His gaze narrowed on me, and he slowly shook his head as one of his hands slid from my shoulder down to my ass. He cupped the cheek and gave it a kneading squeeze.

"This is still cold. Take your pants off, Shelby. They're preventing you from warming."

He tilted his head as if considering something.

"Underwear, too, so they stay clean."

CHAPTER FIFTEEN

MY EYES NEARLY POPPED OUT OF MY HEAD.

"I don't know what you think is going to happen, but I'm not taking off my clothes." I turned to look at Turik, feeling more than a little panicked. "I'm not having sex."

Turik, who'd been watching us while he fed the fire, shot Vorx an annoyed glare before focusing on me.

"Vorx will only warm you. But even then, having his cock nestled against the curve of your pretty ass, especially if you wiggle, will likely push him too far." Turik shrugged lightly. "I had the same problem when you fell asleep on me. I didn't mean to come in your hair, but having your breath warm me there simply felt too good."

Did Turik seriously want me to believe that just holding me naked would be enough to make Vorx come? Based on Turik's expression, yes.

The open admission and frank acknowledgment of what would happen calmed my panic and stroked my ego more than it should have. Inside, I preened just a little, which only encouraged me more.

I turned back to Vorx and considered him and his suggestion for a moment.

"Let me get this straight. I'm supposed to take my pants off all in the name of warming me up, but it will probably result in you coming on me. That about right?"

"Yes."

"I don't really see where the benefit is to me. I'm warm enough." But even as I said it, I reached for my leggings and started tugging them down along with my underwear. Though I would never admit it aloud, there absolutely was a benefit. It was called fun-sexy-time, and it had been far too long since I felt sexy or desired.

As soon as I had everything down, Vorx spun me around and lifted me with one arm banding my waist and the other under my breasts. He groaned at the first contact of skin on skin, and I did a little too. His heat licked at my skin in more than one way as he nestled his cock between my cheeks. The hand at my waist slid down to my hip so he could press against me more firmly.

I blinked at Turik, who was watching us.

"Yep," I managed in a raw whisper. "He's warming my backside."

Turik's mouth twitched a little, and his gaze went to the blanket draped over my shoulders which was now gaping to give him a view of everything.

"Loosen your hold, Vorx. She is still bruised there and needs more care."

Vorx's hold immediately slackened, and I slipped down a little in his grip. The hand on my ribs skidded along my skin until it caught on my breast. I squirmed in his hold as a jolt of heat flared to life inside me, unintentionally rubbing against his hard length still wedged against my backside.

He grunted and shuttled his hips forward with a harsh rasp. The gentle way he held me, along with his obvious wish for more contact, goaded me, and I arched back. His low chuckle brought a small smile to my face, and I set my hands on his forearms.

"Pretty, cold, Shelby," he whispered close to my ear. "I will warm you."

He slid his hand from my hip to cup me between the legs, positioning me more securely against his torso. The heat of his hand branded me, bolting to my core. My lips parted in surprise, and my pulse sped.

"Her cheeks are flushed. Do you hear her heart? She likes your method of warming better than my first attempt. Which doesn't count."

My gaze locked with Turik again.

"I will make your heart race even faster when I warm you," he promised, flashing a smile at me before scowling at Vorx. "She's warm, and it's too cold for her to wash in the lake. Let her go before you spill all over her pretty, soft ass."

Vorx jerked behind me and grunted a pained sound a second before liquid heat painted my spine. Jet after jet coated my skin. I flushed hotter and tried not to squirm against the hand still cupping my mound or the one finger that, with just a bit more pressure, could part me and—

Nope. Not going there.

Instead, I narrowed my eyes at Turik.

"You did that on purpose, mentioning my ass. You wanted him to do that."

Turik chuckled. "Maybe Vorx's warming wasn't so good after all?"

Vorx kissed the back of my head.

"Do not worry, *my* Shelby," Vorx said, releasing me. "I will clean the mess I made." A soft cloth touched my back in brief gentle swipes as Vorx efficiently removed the evidence of how much he enjoyed warming me. When he finished, he tugged my pants back up into place.

"It is a beautiful backside," he said with one more kiss on the back of my head before leaving the cabin.

"I can't decide if you guys are making things weird or interesting."

"Interesting," Turik said without hesitation. "And safe. That more than anything."

Shaking my head at his turned back, I tugged my shirt into place, then shuffled closer to the stove. Although there was heat radiating from the open door, it wasn't enough to dispel the deep chill that had settled into the space from months of disuse.

"Thank you for lighting the fire."

"You're welcome. Are you ready to fish?" he asked, standing and zipping my jacket for me. "You can warm up in here again before we leave."

I nodded and held still as he tucked some stray hair up into my hat.

Impulsively, I wrapped my arms around his waist and hugged him. He held me close, his hands smoothing over my back.

"It does feel safe. And weird. And interesting. But a little confusing too. Games are always fun until someone gets hurt, you know?" I tipped my head to look up at him. "I don't want anyone getting hurt."

He placed a gentle kiss on my forehead then another one a little to the left of that.

"No one will, my Shelby. Trust me. Trust Vorx. We're good at games and would never hurt you."

"What if this game hurts one of you? And I'm not talking about physical injuries here. I'm talking about a hurt heart."

Turik slowly shook his head at me.

"Watching you laugh and smile will never hurt our hearts. It makes us happy too."

I grinned into his chest while calling myself seven shades of stupid for buying into his pretty words. Playing naked games with these two fey had only one outcome, and I didn't relish the idea of breaking someone's heart when they decided it was time to choose between the two of them. But I didn't want to be the adult and call it quits either.

In the last hour, I hadn't thought of Nat once. I hadn't felt fear. In fact, by some miracle, I had actually felt a small measure of joy, and I wanted more—so much more—before I did the mature thing and said stop.

"Okay. Then, I guess I'll keep playing along."

He tipped my chin up and lightly kissed my forehead.

"Good."

After we joined the others outside, I fished my heart out, catching more largemouth bass, which seemed to be a thing for the area. It was fun listening to the fey heckle each other regarding the size versus the quality of their fish. Their friendly, competitive nature made for an enjoyable afternoon.

When it was time to leave, I warmed up in the cabin under Vorx and Turik's close supervision. All my clothes stayed on this time, which I appreciated since I was still a little conflicted about being the center of their game.

We arrived at Tolerance just before dark and parted ways with the rest of the group after promising to go out again in the morning. Even though Turik was eager to get me home for his attempt to warm my frozen legs, I insisted on going to Ryan's for an update on the new safe zone.

Richard answered the door and ushered us inside.

"Good to see you again, Shelby. Turik. Vorx. What brings you by?"

"I wanted to check in to see if there's been any news from Ryan."

"He just got back from Mya's and is in his war room. Come on."

"War room?" I asked as I followed him.

"That's what it looks like with all his maps and drawings." Richard chuckled. "The kid loves a good plan."

"My planning skills are from you," Ryan called as we approached. He looked up at me with an excited grin. "I heard that you took a group out to scout fishing holes. Any luck?"

"Yep. I have two lakes marked. They're a decent size, so farming some fish to restock a pond closer shouldn't hurt anything. Did you find any people when you went back?" I asked, getting to the point.

Ryan shook his head. "We looked in all the houses—top to bottom. I called out with my usual speech about food, safety, and stuff, but there was nothing. We did find the house the hellhound had been in." He frowned slightly. "It looked like the majority of the infected had been on the main floor, and the hound had been in the basement with a smaller group of infected. Based on the evidence—blood and tracks—it looks like some of the infected had fled out the basement window and run away from the house instead of joining the attack. Not a fan of the idea that a few of them had fled like that. Their growing intelligence is making it harder to plan how to handle things."

"Son, no matter how much you plan, you can't control everything," Richard said. "Trying to will drive you nuts."

"Right," Ryan said. "So I'm focusing on what I can control. Eden's subdivision is as perfect as she said. There are about fifty houses clustered around a pond big enough to support more fish. There's a fair number of trees planted along the streets, but fields border the subdivision. It's far enough from the highway not to be seen. All the homes are on their own septic and wells. A few have solar and woodstoves. I have some fey out dismantling solar systems we've marked. I have scouts looking for more. The main group is moving cars from the highway to the new place. They're familiar with how to build the wall, but because it's farther away from us, they'll make it thicker and taller. Just in case."

"Are they going to include some field space inside the walls?" I asked. "It would give room for protected planting or building more homes."

He pulled out a sketch of the area and the placement of the wall he told them to build. He had included enough field space on all sides to provide a buffer between homes and walls. The open ground could easily be used for growing crops.

"Mom mentioned doing a cut out in the wall and expanding it for an orchard and bees, but I'm worried about putting too much in one place. We have the humans in Tenacity, most of the livestock in Tolerance, and vegetables in this new place."

"You're right. It wouldn't hurt to look for another place. If you truly want to integrate humans and fey, the best way to do it is with this co-op living. It would force trade and mingling.

Plus, there are a lot of people cramped into homes over in Tenacity who might be ready to consider a different lifestyle."

Ryan leaned back in his chair, his gaze holding mine.

"Is it weird, platonically living with two fey?"

I struggled not to flush and nodded.

"It's a little weird. Especially the platonic part. But I think it's working well."

"It's working very well," Turik said. "Shelby already feels safer with us. Soon she will be ready to—"

"Stop," Ryan said, holding up his hand.

"Yeah, you've hit the weird part," I said.

Turik's hand settled on my shoulder, and I struggled to maintain eye contact with Ryan as he gave me a wry look.

"We'll need to make sure all parties clearly understand the intent behind the co-ed housing. That it's not meant for a quick hookup but building better relations and maybe even some friendships."

"Yeah, that might be a good idea," I said weakly.

CHAPTER SIXTEEN

"ARE YOU SURE YOU'RE WARM ENOUGH?" TURIK ASKED YET AGAIN.

"Look at my face. It's still on fire. Trust me. I am plenty warm. Just what exactly were you going to say to Ryan? 'Soon Shelby will be ready to have my babies?' You can't go around telling people stuff like that. It makes them uncomfortable. Embarrasses them. And embarrassed people will want to avoid you. Do you want people avoiding you?"

"No."

"Then practice some discretion." I rubbed a hand over my face. "This is my fault. I shouldn't have let Vorx warm me up. It's sending all the wrong messages. You—"

Turik stepped in front of me. The sudden press of his chest against my face stopped my tirade and my annoyed pacing.

"Quiet and listen for a moment, Shelby," Turik said, not unkindly. "Vorx and I were both there that night. We saw the hopelessness in your eyes. Hopelessness that *he* put there." Turik lightly ran his hand over my bruised middle, as if I had any doubt about whom he was referring to.

"You will not be ready for my babies soon. I know this," he

continued. "But, perhaps, with Vorx and me, you will soon be ready to see a better future than the one you saw only a few days ago. A future that is not filled with fear but with your smiles and laughter. That is all I was going to tell Ryan."

I huffed out a breath, my annoyance fading to make room for some guilt, and wrapped my arms around Turik's waist.

"Besides, I am too smart to tell more men about your perfect, soft body. Vorx is already too focused on your sweet backside." Turik's hands slid around to cup my ass and lift me so his hard length pressed against the apex of my thighs. "Your front is just as pretty."

"You're ridiculous! Does everything lead back to sex with you?"

"No," Vorx said from his place on the couch where he was watching us. "Sometimes it leads to food. Check to see if she has a fever. She's forgetting things we already told her."

I batted Turik's hand away when he tried and rolled my eyes at Vorx. "You know damn well that there's nothing wrong with my mind. But I'm starting to question both of yours. Put me down."

Turik reluctantly did so.

"Are you angry?" he asked.

"No. Annoyed."

He flashed a grin at me, which let me know that my annoyance didn't bother him in the least. Deciding to self-soothe, I pivoted and went to the kitchen to raid the cupboard for junk food.

As soon as I had a bag of chips in hand, though, I sighed. We hadn't had dinner yet, and it would be smarter for me to make something healthy instead of munching on snack foods. I didn't want to be smart, but with both of them scrutinizing my current state of mind, that was the route I chose.

I rummaged through the cabinets for dinner ingredients. However, before I could grab the pan, Turik tugged me to the couch and handed me the chips.

"Sit," Vorx said. "Relax and enjoy your crisps. I will make us something to eat while Turik rubs your feet."

Surprised, I watched Vorx retreat to the kitchen. At least, I did until I caught the way Turik was observing me.

"What?"

"Do you not want me to rub your feet again?" He gestured to the couch in question.

The remnants of annoyance evaporated like it had never existed, and I quickly sat sideways on the cushions, lifting my legs so Turik could sit under me.

The next forty minutes were bliss. Not only did Turik rub my feet, but when I groaned, he also included my calves. While he turned my muscles to mush, I idly nibbled on chips and inhaled the scent of whatever meaty goodness Vorx was cooking up in the kitchen.

"I'm feeling decidedly spoiled and like it a lot," I said.

"Good," Vorx said from the kitchen. "Then you'll stay."

I shook my head at both of them. They were so focused on my happiness that I couldn't help but wonder if I was worth their effort. Not that I didn't value myself. Quite the opposite. I was reclaiming my self-value with a vengeance, which is why I told Turik I wasn't ready for kids. I needed to find myself first. Wouldn't they rather chase a woman who was ready to jump into a relationship with them, though? I recalled Turik's comment about females running away and realized I might actually be the better option. I wasn't running. Hell, no. Minus the embarrassing moments, I loved living with them.

After Vorx said dinner was ready, we ate together and watched a movie. It didn't feel weird to sit between them and rest my head against Turik's thigh while he brushed and braided my hair and Vorx rubbed my legs. There wasn't anything sexual about the way they cared for me. I felt cherished and coddled, but I knew very well they would make it sexual if I was willing.

When it was time for bed, I went to Turik's room to change and brush my teeth but didn't bother trying his bed again. I knew where I wanted to be.

Turik was on his usual side when I entered their bedroom. He flashed his teeth at me and pulled back the covers. I quickly got in, relishing his warmth and the comfort of his presence.

Across the hall, the bathroom door opened. A moment later, Vorx's shadowy form filled the doorway.

"Good," he said. "I hate listening to your restless loneliness."

I made a face as he settled into his place and turned his head to brush his lips against my temple.

"Sleep, Shelby."

"You should try being less bossy," I said, rolling away from him to toss an arm over Turik's waist. "Or haven't you heard? You can catch more flies with honey than vinegar."

Vorx grunted, and someone's fingers toyed with my braid. It felt like Turik, which suited me fine.

Lonely. Pfft. Vorx was mistaking the need to be left alone with loneliness.

Exhaling softly, I rubbed my cheek against Turik's pectoral

and closed my eyes. I was just here because it was more comfortable, and I felt safer. That was it.

"IT'S difficult to hold still when she does this," Vorx said, his voice a tortured rumble.

"Think of other things. She will not be happy if she wakes with sticky hair," Turik answered, sounding entirely unlike himself.

Their conversation penetrated the fog in my mind and almost had me bolting upright...until I realized my position. Someone had his hard length nestled against my ass. The other hard length was wedged under my cheek...and I was rubbing my face on it.

"There is no damn way I did this to myself," I mumbled, lifting my head to confirm I was laying across Vorx with my butt against Turik. "Someone was touching me. Moving me in my sleep. Admit it."

Both fey blinked at me. Sweat beaded their foreheads, and their hands were tucked behind their heads. It should have looked like a carefree, relaxed pose, but I was pretty sure Turik was fisting his hair.

"You know what? Never mind. I don't want to talk about whatever this is." I scrambled off the bed. "Or talk to either of you for the rest of the day."

I practically ran from the room and didn't stop until I was safely locked away in Turik's bathroom. There, I set my flushed forehead against the cool glass of the mirror and glared at the self-deluded woman, who still couldn't face her reality.

As much as I wanted to blame them for the position in

which I'd woken, I knew better. That was on me. I'd gone to bed with them, and I'd woken in a similar position with them before. Just not at the same time. What did snuggling like that in my sleep say about me? Probably nothing more than yesterday's warm-up session said.

I was starved for positive affection. I wanted to feel good with someone again, fading bruises be damned. How messed up was that?

Moving away from the mirror, I rubbed a hand over my face and tried to get my thoughts straight for the day. Fishing. Scouting ponds for resources. That I could do. I could be useful. Helpful even.

With my clothes on.

After brushing my teeth, I layered strategically, to avoid getting so cold, then reluctantly joined Vorx and Turik in the kitchen. A plate of eggs and toast waited for me on the counter, and two very stoic fey stood by the door.

They let me eat in silence and didn't try to help me with my shoes or jacket when I finished.

I didn't like it. I felt hollow without their conversation and attentiveness.

Lonely.

I made an annoyed sound and glared at Vorx before stomping out the door.

Neither fey spoke to me as I strode down the street, heading for the canoes. They did, however, quietly converse with the fey who joined us along the way, which only annoyed me further. I hated that I felt so needy and attention starved. What was wrong with me? Hadn't I just run from a man who had given me all sorts of the wrong kind of attention? Why would I want anyone's attention? Why couldn't I just lay in bed by myself and just go to sleep?

Allowing myself a moment of frank honesty, I acknowledged Vorx's wise words from the night before. I was lonely. Deeply, disturbingly clingy, kind of lonely. I wanted someone to kiss my forehead and hold me just like Turik had said my first day here. I just hadn't recognized how badly until they'd both started doing it. And I wanted more. Kindness. Gentle touches. Caring. And above all, the solid protection of Vorx and Turik.

And while a small part of me felt conflicted about both of them paying attention to me, the other part knew that it wasn't a big deal. At least, not to them. They were competitive by nature and made a game out of some of the attention, and the rest they gave willingly because they genuinely cared about me as a person. They both understood that I wasn't looking for anything more at this point.

So, what harm was there in waking up with my face pressed against Vorx's balls and my crack riding Turik's shaft?

None.

I chewed on my bottom lip and immediately regretted the way I'd stormed out of the room and my continued pouting. My first reaction should have been an apology. Apologizing after the fact now sucked, which is why I continued to wait until most of the fey were distracted with gathering canoes.

Turik and Vorx stood on each side of me, watching me more than their brothers. I reached out and slipped my gloved hands into theirs.

"I'm sorry," I said softly. "I shouldn't have tried blaming you for something that was obviously all me. Apparently, I'm restless, no matter where I sleep." I glanced at both of them sheepishly. "I'll try to come up with a better plan for tonight."

"No," Vorx said firmly. "I want nothing to change." He released my hand to cradle the back of my head and set his forehead to mine. "I want you to feel safe."

I exhaled slowly, closing my eyes and absorbing his presence. The strength he emanated wrapped around me, an extra layer of the protection he was so determined to give.

When he freed me, Turik picked me up and pressed his lips to my cheek and the corner of my eye.

"I want nothing to change as well, my Shelby. We only wish for you to be safe and happy."

I snuggled against his chest and whispered my thanks as he jogged after our canoe carriers.

The group already knew the location for the next lake and headed in that direction once we cleared the wall. It took much longer to reach our destination and, despite my layers, I was cold and stiff when we arrived at the water's edge.

"There is a house over there," Vorx said.

I didn't play stupid or balk at what I knew was coming. Instead, I quietly shivered in Turik's arms while two other fey cleared the house.

The moment they gave the go-ahead, Turik looked down at me, his gaze filled with hunger.

"Will you allow me to warm you, my Shelby?"

A flush ignited my cheeks as I nodded.

"It's only fair to give you your chance, right?" I murmured.

Vorx chuckled as he followed us inside.

CHAPTER SEVENTEEN

I shivered and wondered what level of insanity Turik had planned as I stripped and watched Vorx arrange the blankets on the floor in front of the fireplace. Turik straightened away from the small flames he'd managed.

"Lie down," he said.

Wearing only my bra and underwear, I dove for the cold blankets.

"This is w-worse."

"It won't be." He loosened his leather pants and slid them down his thighs, freeing his already semi-hard length.

My gaze locked on his impressive shaft, and heat began to pool in my middle. Was that how he planned to warm me? A strip-tease? It was kind of working. Swallowing hard, I watched him step out of his pants and toss them aside.

Vorx moved to the fireplace and took over feeding the flames, doing his part to try to warm me, which I appreciated. I needed all the help I could get. My toes felt like ice blocks.

When Turik joined me under the covers, it was impossible not to immediately move closer to the waves of delicious heat that radiated off of his skin. However, I was so cold, it wasn't enough.

He took charge of the situation and gripped my arms, suddenly hauling me up and over.

"What are you—ah!"

I landed sprawled on top of him, my legs spread slightly.

"Wrap your arms and legs around me. Skin to skin. Use my warmth."

Still trying to process all the hard muscle underneath me, especially the one pulsing against my lower stomach, I slowly rested my cheek on his sternum. He grunted at the cold contact.

"Sorry."

"I like when you warm yourself on me. Even your cold hands."

I grinned a little, remembering how I'd warmed them the previous day. Partially straddling his hips, I slid my hands to his sides and listened to his hissed-out breaths. My grin widened a bit more.

"I think I like warming myself on you too," I admitted.

As my hands searched out new warm spots, his shaft twitched underneath me. Small moves that called attention to his impressive size. The heat in my middle grew at the thought of sliding up his torso into a more comfortable position—one that would better align us, if not for my underwear.

His hands settled on my lower back, warming the skin there before slowly gliding down to massage some warmth into my backside. Each gentle rotation nudged me up a bit farther, feeding my fantasy until I couldn't ignore my need to grind myself against him.

Heart thumping, I pressed my hands against his chest and dragged myself up his torso, skin to skin, not stopping until I aligned his cock against my core. He grunted, and his hands gripped my hips more firmly as I gave an experimental rotation.

A burst of hot pleasure coursed through me, and I forced myself to still. The hot throb of his length continued to twitch against me.

"How is your pussy that warm?" he asked, arching against me before catching himself and settling into place. "Sorry." He returned his hands to my back and continued rubbing the skin there.

"Ghua said that Eden's pussy is always warmer than the rest of her," Vorx said from his place by the fire. "It must be a female thing."

Turning my head to warm the other cheek, I met Vorx's gaze and chuckled.

"It's a core temperature thing. Outer extremities cool first. When the core starts cooling, then you're looking at hypothermia, which is really bad."

Turik moved underneath me again. A slow arch that rubbed against my clit just the right way.

"She opened her mouth a little, and her eyes dilated. Repeat whatever you did," Vorx said, surprising me.

Before I could protest, Turik arched into me again, and I almost groaned.

"Does it warm you when I do this, Shelby?" Turik said, continuing his steady rock.

"Yeah." The word was strangled, like my hold on Turik's sides.

"Good. I like pussy-cock hugs."

I snorted with laughter and rotated my hips against his next arch. We both moaned then. His grip on my waist changed. It wasn't firmer—he was very careful even though the bruises were fading more every day. No, it was a slight tilt in his grip as if he was encouraging me to sit up and ride his temptingly obscene length.

How long had it been since I'd come? Ages. Ages and ages.

The memory of Nat rose up in my mind from when he still had been pretending to be loving, and I inwardly cringed. I hated that he was my last orgasm memory, not that I was ready to try to overwrite it. Turik's light petting was enough for now. Enough to warm me and remind me that being with someone else could feel good.

I rubbed my face against his skin and breathed him in as he continued to rock against me. Each brush of his shaft against my clit had me wondering if light petting was the correct assessment, though. The fire that had sparked to life earlier grew in heat and ferocity until the flames licked my insides. I pushed away from his chest, bracing my hands on his chiseled torso as I arched my back and ground down against each of his thrusts.

A fine coating of sweat dampened my skin. I closed my eyes, chasing after that elusive jump into oblivion. And when I found it, I tumbled headfirst.

The high, soft wail that ripped from me echoed in the space along with Turik's harsh breathing. A moment later, he grunted, and his shaft jumped underneath me. I opened my eyes in time to see rope after rope of white paint his abdomen.

Our eyes locked as he finished. His pupils were fully blown, and his ears stained a dark grey.

"I'm not sure if I owe you another apology or a thank you," I said, my heart still racing away.

"Neither," Turik answered. "I am the one who owes you

both. Thank you for letting me warm you. I am sorry for releasing, though. Pussy-cock hugs while you make happy noises..." He shook his head slowly. "There is no greater pleasure."

I wondered what kind of reaction he would have to actual sex.

"I will go clean up. Here," he said, gently lifting me.

Another set of hands gripped my arms and plucked me the rest of the way off of Turik. Vorx sat on the blanket pile with me, his chest warming my back as Turik rose and walked away. How far I'd taken things registered a few minutes too late, and I twisted to look up at Vorx.

"I'm so sorry. I—"

"You owe me no apology either. Turik warmed you much better than I did and won this round fairly," Vorx said. "I will work harder next time."

A sputtered laugh rippled out of me as I shook my head in disbelief. I should have known his response to dry humping with Turik in front of him would be the equivalent of a shoulder shrug.

He smiled down at me before picking up a blanket and wrapping it around us. Too content to move, I melted against his chest and closed my eyes. The orgasm had been well needed and earned, and I still felt pleasant little aftershocks zinging through me.

My pulse gradually returned to normal enough that I opened my eyes and looked at my pile of clothes. I knew I should get dressed, but it was just so comfortable in Vorx's arms. And the view...

Built higher on the shoreline, the cabin's main floor boasted floor-to-ceiling windows on either side of the massive fireplace.

From where I lay, I had a perfect view of the other side of the lake. The beauty of the dark, barren branches, the crisp blue sky, and the thin strip of white coating the opposite shore spoke of calm vacation days gone by.

I exhaled peacefully then jerked in Vorx's hold when my gaze caught on movement.

"There's something on the opposite shore," I said.

He turned his head and followed my gaze.

"It looks like an infected. Get dressed."

Turik emerged from the bathroom and grabbed his pants as Vorx helped me up.

"Do you see more than one?" he asked Vorx as I rushed to redress.

"No, but the trees are thick behind him."

Turik grunted.

"What does one mean?" I asked. "What do we do?"

"It means we are done fishing and will return to Tolerance."

I was up in his arms the moment I had my jacket zipped and out the door seconds later. Vorx motioned to the rest of the fey, and they immediately gathered everything.

We left the lake at a run, and Turik pressed a kiss to my temple.

"You are safe, my Shelby. You will see."

Weirdly, I felt safe. Maybe it was the afterglow of the orgasm I'd just had, but I wasn't afraid. The logical part of my brain knew I should be, though. An infected sighting was never a good thing. But safely in Turik's arms, it didn't seem like a bad thing either.

What little warmth I'd managed during our time at the cabin quickly dissipated due to the speed we traveled. I did my best to press against Turik and steal what I could from him, knowing that it would be dangerous to stop.

Yet, that was exactly what we did, but not due to me.

Several miles from home, one of the forerunners spotted a few infected hiding behind trees. The way the infected peeked around the trunks, using them as shields, was freaky as hell. But the small group wasn't anything the forerunners couldn't handle.

However, before we could move on, distant gunshots rang out.

"Ryan said we should note the location of any humans we found," Turik said, looking at me. "Will you worry about the humans if we leave now?"

It was no mystery that humans fired those shots. The infected hadn't evolved to that level—something I prayed would never happen—and the fey didn't use guns. If the humans were shooting, that meant they were in trouble.

"I will worry. But I'll also worry if any of you go. Bullets can kill you."

A few of the fey chuckled.

"We are very fast, Shelby, and know how to not be seen," Vorx said.

I gave the group a hesitant look.

"No one gets hurt."

A few of our group grunted and left. I shivered as I stared after them.

"They can find us in Tolerance and share the news of what they found there," Turik said. "You're too cold to stay outside." He took off running again.

However, the group rejoined us a few minutes later and said they found more infected not far from where we'd been.

Apparently, the humans had fired the shots and ran off before the fey had arrived.

My thoughts immediately turned to Nat, and Turik seemed to notice because he pressed a kiss to my temple and murmured that I was safe.

"I know I am." I snuggled against him and petted his chest, hoping he would know I did believe him. It just didn't remove all worry.

Arriving home blood-splattered with the canoes didn't draw any extra attention. It was just another business-as-usual day, and I was kind of glad for that. There were no delays getting back to the house.

"Do we need to tell someone about the infected sighting at the lake or the gunshots?" I asked, shivering as Turik unzipped my jacket and tugged off my sweater.

"No. Our brothers will let Drav know," Vorx said, answering me before looking at Turik. "I'll warm her in the shower while you make her something to eat."

Turik grunted, and I found myself in Vorx's arms between one heartbeat and the next.

"What about your stitches? They shouldn't get wet, should they? And don't I have a say in any of this?"

"Of course you do. If you prefer I warm you the same way Turik did, I am willing. Pussy-cock hugging looked enjoyable."

He shot me a sly grin, and I shook my head.

CHAPTER EIGHTEEN

HE CONTINUED TO THE BATHROOM AND SAT ME ON THE COUNTER.

"Stay."

"I'm not a dog," I said, giving his back a glare when he turned away to start the shower.

"If you were, you would not be shaking with cold. Let me help you, Shelby."

He said it so reasonably that I stayed on the counter and waited. As soon as the water was on, he faced me. The hunger in his hooded gaze, which lingered on my face, set off another shiver.

"Are you sure this is about warming me?"

"Yes. And proving I am better at it than Turik."

His cocky smirk did me in. When he reached out for my foot, I lifted it willingly and watched him remove first one sock then the other. His fingers brushed my right arch, and an involuntary giggle escaped me.

"Ticklish," I said.

He grunted, tossed my socks aside, and nudged my legs wide to step between them. I stared up into his gold and green eyes, feeling that curl of anticipation gathering in my middle as he eased my shirt over my head. His touch skimmed up my arms, setting off another wave of shivers, before he reached behind me and removed my bra.

He didn't grab for me or leer at what he uncovered. But he did glance. The desire in that one look heated my blood, and I could tell by how he quickly focused on my jeans that he wanted to do more than simply look. His attempt at detachment made me want him to do so much more.

In that sexy one-handed move some men could master, he removed his own shirt and tossed it aside. I cleared my throat at the rippling display of muscle and focused on the stitches over his ribs.

"I was serious about the stitches. Can you get them wet?" I asked as steam filled the room.

"They need to come out. I think a shower will make that easier."

"But what does Cassie think?"

He shrugged and reached for the button of my jeans. Oh, the things it did to me to watch him undo them. With my jeans open, he met my gaze again and waited for me to make the next move. I set my hands on the counter and hooked my bare feet around his hips.

The smirk curving his lips stole my breath while the man stole the rest of my clothes.

While my blood ran hot, the stone counter still felt warmer than my bare ass when he set me down again. But not by much. And that difference dwindled further when he removed his own pants, showing off the massive erection he sported.

I couldn't look away. As Turik had said, the two of them were equally matched physically.

"Are you warm, Shelby?" Vorx asked.

There were parts of me that were heating, but those didn't count. So, I slowly shook my head.

A smile tugged at Vorx's lips as he held out his hand.

"Will you allow me to warm you?"

"Yes." I placed my hand in his, and a rumble of satisfaction echoed from him as he led me into the shower.

Soothing steam surrounded me. That alone would've been enough to warm me, but I knew Vorx had bigger plans. After all, he couldn't do things by half measures if he wanted to one-up Turik's official first attempt, which had ended quite well, in my opinion.

Vorx backed me into the water and gently wet my hair. I held still as he massaged my scalp and worked his strong fingers down my neck. I wanted to moan with pleasure in a completely different way this time. How long had it been since someone had taken this much time to care for me? And to this level? Never.

He continued down to my shoulders, melting away any tension I might've still carried from our run-in with the infected. I sighed and leaned my forehead against Vorx's sternum while lightly anchoring my hands at his sides.

His muscles jumped under my touch.

In a moment of complete self-honesty, I acknowledged just how much I craved this. It was more than physical contact and an amusing game between friends. I craved Vorx's undivided attention. I craved his touch. I craved meaning something to someone. Something positive and caring versus all the hate and pain I'd suffered because of Nat.

However, I couldn't help but wonder what my cravings

meant since I didn't just crave those things from Vorx. I craved it all from Turik too.

Equally.

And while they didn't mind sharing me now, I was adult enough to acknowledge that this couldn't continue forever. Eventually, when they decided on a winner for their competition, they would want me to choose between the two of them. And I wasn't ready for that kind of relationship yet.

The current one was more than confusing enough—like how it didn't bother me that I'd orgasmed with Turik in front of Vorx or how Vorx was likely going to try to one-up that experience with another orgasm now. In fact, I was looking forward to that part.

The confusing part was what I felt about both of them. Again, equally. Affection. Need in all the ways I'd already acknowledged. And I wasn't sure what else. Not that Vorx was about to let my confusion morph into anything stressful.

His hands methodically massaged their way down my back inch by inch. By the time he reached the base of my spine, he held me flush to his front since his magic touch melted all of my strength. I couldn't even contain the small sounds escaping my lips, a sign of how much I liked what he was doing.

Those sounds became more urgent when his hands slipped to my ass and he began kneading the muscle there. A soft growl rumbled in his chest, and his erection twitched against my stomach.

"You are so soft here."

"I'm soft everywhere compared to you."

"I like your softness."

My pulse sped further, and a bolt of need struck my middle. Like I had with Turik, I took the step from passive game participant to active player and leaned forward to lick a drop of water from his chest before meeting his gaze.

"Then maybe you should massage a few other soft places."

The words had barely left my mouth when he spun me around and pressed my back to his front. I sputtered against a face full of spray for only a moment before he turned us.

The rumble of his laughter registered a half-second after I finished sputtering. Instead of getting mad, I laughed too.

"I'm guessing drowning me wasn't part of your 'warm her better than Turik' plan, was it?"

"No, it was not. This was, though."

He covered one of my breasts with his hand, and the heat of his palm branded the flesh he began kneading. My nipple pebbled, and I bit back a groan.

"I can hear what this does to your heart. How it races." He rolled my nipple between his fingers while the other hand drifted down to cup me between the legs.

"Turik seemed surprised by the heat of your pussy when it was hugging his cock. But this doesn't feel shockingly hot," he said, adding pressure against my folds. "I don't think you're warm enough yet. Do you?"

I shook my head and let it fall back against his chest.

"Good."

That rumbled word sounded more like a purr and sent a shiver of anticipation through me.

He lifted me higher, alternating between toying with my nipple and kneading my breast. I was so focused on that sensation I wasn't altogether paying attention to everything else until I felt his hard length stroking against my ass.

"You are still cold here," he said, arching against me. "That is no good."

He arched again, this time with more force. The long slide of his shaft parting my ass cheeks made my eyes go wide.

Vorx hissed out a breath and shifted his hold on my front to lift me higher. One of his fingers slipped into my folds and pressed against the side of my clit. A whimper escaped me, and I wiggled against the digit. Whether to escape it or for more, I wasn't sure.

Vorx rumbled with amusement.

"Is this what you wish for?" he asked, his lips skimming my ear as his finger continued to explore the center of my pleasure. "Such a small thing. I saw it when you knelt on the bed. A pretty pink bit peeking from your pussy. I want a closer look, but not now. Now, I want to hear your happy noises while your beautiful, soft curves hug my cock."

My core clenched at his words. Then he moved us, lifting me and arching his hips so his hard length slicked through the curves he adored. I could feel the bumps and ridges sliding against my back hole, and when he lifted me high enough to feel his thick head rub there in a dangerously forbidden way, my pulse stuttered. A satisfied rumble echoed from his chest. He repeated the move at the same time he pinched my clit.

Sparks exploded behind my eyelids, and I screamed out my orgasm, pressing back as he continued to shuttle his length against me.

"Good, Shelby," he said roughly. "But you're not warm enough yet, are you?"

His finger slid to my entrance and thrust inside. An incoherent sound left me, and I gripped his forearms as I held on for the ride of my life. He was unrelenting in his pursuit of my pleasure and didn't find his own release until he made me scream again.

The second orgasm left me rung-out and limp against his chest.

"I love the sounds you make. Will you make them for me again?"

I weakly shook my head, and he chuckled. "I think you will. But not yet."

Supporting my weight, he turned me and started rinsing my back. When his fingers swept to the place only I washed, I shivered.

"Did you like the feel of me here?" he asked.

I didn't answer. I couldn't. Yes, I'd liked it. Far too much. And I worried that, if I admitted it, he would put things in places that weren't ready for his level of intrusion. So I kept quiet, which only incited him to clean the curves that fascinated him for a little longer.

My pulse returned to normal, and I could almost stand on my own by the time he turned off the water. Turik was waiting with a towel and started drying me off while Vorx dried himself.

"Did I warm you?" Vorx asked.

"Yes. I was very warm."

"Warmer than Turik made you?"

I groaned. "I don't want to be the judge. I'm already the challenge."

"No, Shelby," Turik said, gently tipping my chin up. "You're the prize."

Then he leaned in and peppered my face with light kisses until I was grinning like an idiot.

Smiling, he pulled back from me and glanced at Vorx.

"This one goes to you. She made more happy sounds here than in the cottage."

"She likes when I focus on her soft backside. Ass-cock hugs are good, but I still want to feel a pussy-cock hug."

The spark of interest in Turik's eyes had me holding up my hand. "No more cock hugs are needed. I'm warm, and I'm hungry. And you already rang the bell for this round. It goes to Vorx." I patted Turik's hard chest and gave him a consoling look. "Sorry."

He grinned at me.

"I will try harder next time."

I wasn't sure if I would survive much harder.

CHAPTER NINETEEN

TURIK FINISHED DRYING ME AND INSISTED ON BRUSHING MY HAIR. Vorx leaned in the doorway, watching us and giving Turik suggestions on braid patterns. The comfortable companionship they shared only relaxed me further.

When my hair braids achieved their desired look, the three of us went to the kitchen and put together a simple lunch of soup and crackers.

"You should have more than soup," Vorx said as he pulled a bag of chips from the cupboard and a box of snack cakes.

"Trust me. This is already more than I'm used to and plenty."

His gaze flicked to my hips, and my mouth dropped open as I understood his intention.

"Are you trying to fatten me up?"

"Yes."

I grinned at him. "So you're obviously an ass man. What about you, Turik?"

"I'm a pussy man."

Soup went down the wrong tube, and I started choking

through my laughter. Turik grunted and patted my back in concern. Vorx took my soup away from me and handed me a snack cake, which he deemed safer. Right...

When I settled down enough to wipe my tears and draw a decent breath, I reclaimed my soup and clarified my question.

"Men typically find a woman's breasts, butt, or legs more attractive than the rest. Of those three, which attracts you more?"

Turik's gaze dipped to my breasts.

"Well, I guess that's my answer."

Shaking my head at the pair, I finished my soup under their watchful gazes, ate a snack cake just to listen to Vorx's rumble of pleasure, then curled up on the couch and patted the cushions on each side of me.

"Since fishing is out for today, how about a movie while we digest? Then we can find something else to do."

"Something outside so you get cold," Turik said, sitting on my right.

I grinned and leaned into him, enjoying the way he wrapped his arm around me and pulled me close. Vorx sat to my left and drew my legs up into his lap. His hands drifted up my jean-clad thighs to the curve of my hip. Three orgasms in one day, and I still felt a renewed rush of heat in my middle at the obvious sign of his obsession with that part of my body.

"Another warm-up session later might not be the worst idea," I said with a smirk.

Turik rumbled under me and kissed my temple.

"Pussy-cock hugs are the best ideas," Turik said.

"Ass-cock hugs too," Vorx added.

"Pfft. If 'hugs' blew your mind, you're going to love actual intercourse."

Both of them froze.

"I didn't mean...I mean, when you have sex with the girl you choose. I didn't mean me. I'm not choosing between the two of you. That's not what that was. I like you both."

Turik's lips pressed to my hair. "Breathe, Shelby. You're safe. We're not upset. You don't have to choose. You can enjoy spending time with us both."

Glad I hadn't put my foot so far into my mouth that I couldn't remove it, I let out a relieved exhale.

"I just don't want to do anything to ruin this—living here with both of you. I do feel safe and like that I'm able to be myself for the first time in a very long time. I just don't want to lose that." As soon as those words were out of my mouth, I wanted to kick myself. "But that doesn't mean you need to feel obligated to keep me. If either of you meets a female you want to bring home, all you have to do is say the word, and I'll find someone else to take me in."

It wouldn't be easy, not with being exiled from Tenacity still hanging over my head. Sure, the fey didn't seem to care overly much, and Mya had given me her blessing, but I hesitated to believe I could find as friendly of a welcome as I did with Turik and Vorx.

"Agreed?" I pressed when neither of them made a sound.

They shared a look then grunted in their non-committal way.

Before I could press for more, there was a knock on our door. Nervous about having company, I stood when Vorx went to answer it and was grateful I was wearing leggings and a solid shirt. My desperation to make a good impression must have shown on my face because Turik kissed the top of my head and tugged me against his side.

When Vorx opened the door and I saw Drav standing there, my stomach dropped. A visit from the guy in charge couldn't be a good thing.

His gaze swept over the three of us as he entered. He nodded in greeting to the fey before settling his gaze on me.

"Mya thinks the gunshots you heard near the lake might be Nat and his men since Turik mentioned seeing guns when he rescued you. I'm asking for volunteers to search around the lake and want someone who can identify if any humans found are the exiled ones from Tenacity."

"You want me to go?" I asked, surprise lacing my words.

"No," Turik said, his arm tightening around me. "He's asking me to join the group."

I tipped my head to look up at Turik.

The idea of staying here without him, even though I had Vorx, created waves of fear that lapped at my insides. Not that I could say no. Not when Mya and Drav had listened to my warning and were taking me seriously.

"If it's Nat, you'll need to be extra careful," I said, unable to look away from Turik. "Don't let him hurt you. Promise me."

My voice broke at the end, and Turik wrapped me in a hug. I leaned into his embrace, desperate for the contact and the comfort. His hand smoothed over my hair, and he kissed the top of my head.

"Nat can't hurt me, Shelby. You will see. I will return without injury. I'm better than Vorx."

Vorx grunted a laugh, but I couldn't bring myself to smile. Instead, I tightened my death grip around Turik's waist.

"When do we leave?" Turik asked.

"Now, before the humans can go far."

A second later, Vorx untangled me from Turik's hold and hugged me from behind.

"I will keep you safe, Shelby," he said low against my ear. "You have my word."

My worried gaze remained locked on Turik, who leaned in to kiss my forehead. At the last second, I stood on my toes and tipped my head back. Our lips touched, the lightest brush of contact that sent a searing ache to my heart. When he moved to pull back, I took his face in my hands and parted my lips.

He growled and held my face in return. Instead of giving me the ravishing kiss I wanted, he peppered my face with little kisses while Vorx continued to hold me.

"I will return at nightfall," Turik said against my skin. "By dawn at the latest."

"Just be safe," I begged.

He grunted and withdrew.

From the safety of Vorx's arms, I watched Turik leave with Drav. The sound of the door closing behind the pair felt like a hammer to my heart, and I clutched Vorx's forearm covering my waist.

Vorx had barely limped his way home a few days ago. What if the same thing or worse happened to Turik?

"You are worrying again," Vorx said. "Tell me what you fear so I can help."

"That he's going to get hurt and both of you are going to be held together with thread."

Vorx grunted and turned me in his arms.

"Turik is strong and smart. He knows how much this"—he gestured at his side—"upset you and will do everything possible to avoid injury."

That didn't calm my fears, and Vorx knew it, based on his sigh.

"Come," he said, taking my hand and leading me to the door.

"Where are we going?" I asked when he handed me my shoes.

"To Cassie's before my skin grows over the thread holding me together."

I hurried to put my stuff on. Outside, the cold air cleared my head a little and allowed me to think objectively. It was silly to worry about a grown man who'd lived thousands of lifetimes and fought hellhounds during each one of those. He was strong, and he was smart. Obviously, he could handle himself.

Yet, while I knew all that, I still feared losing what I'd found. I wanted to tell myself that meant a safe and happy home, but if that were the case, I wouldn't be worrying so much. Not with Vorx still here, watching over me.

I glanced at the fey walking at my side. He caught my glance and smirked at me.

"Once the stitches are gone, I will show you I can carry you better than Turik."

Unable to help myself, I snorted.

"We don't need to make a game out of carrying me too. I enjoy walking."

Vorx shrugged. "I enjoy touching your soft backside. Which one of us will get our way, do you think?"

I shot him a scowl. "Don't even think about it. Once your stitches are out, you're probably still going to need to take it easy for a while."

Even though I knew the fey healed faster, I honestly didn't think the stitches were ready to come out. However, when we reached Cassie's house, she welcomed us inside with a knowing smile.

"I thought we might see you soon."

Vorx shot me a smirk, and I rolled my eyes at him as Cassie led us back to the room she used for medical purposes.

"Kerr will remove the stitches for you. He'll be right in."

As soon as she left, Vorx stripped off his shirt and dropped his pants. It was so unexpected that I opened my mouth to ask what he was doing, only to stop at the sight of the row of stitches on his thigh. How hadn't I noticed that until now? I remembered a bandage, but not the stitches. We'd even showered together for the love of—

Kerr walked into the room.

"I'll do your side first."

It didn't take long for Kerr to pluck out the sutures he'd placed so carefully. After wiping both areas clean one last time, Kerr dismissed Vorx with a dry, "kill the hound faster next time," and left the room.

"That's it?" I asked as I watched Vorx dress.

"Yes."

I wasn't buying it. There had to be some kind of "take it easy" warning.

When we left the room, I saw Cassie.

"What are his limitations? Maybe don't lift anything over fifty pounds?"

She grinned at me. "Trying to tell them not to do something is like trying to convince a toddler to take a nap. Except Vorx knows his body better than the toddler would."

I opened my mouth to say more, but Vorx picked me up and started for the door.

"Thank you, Cassie," he said just before letting us out.

"Just because you're a difficult patient doesn't mean you were right," I said, crossing my arms and looking up at him.

He smirked down at me and picked up his pace. However, being in our house again brought back the fact that Turik wasn't there.

Although I said nothing and gave Vorx a sweet smile when he helped me out of my jacket, he knew Turik's departure still weighed on me. And all the relaxing baths, desserts, and massages in the world wouldn't have been enough to distract me from my worry. Yet, Vorx still threw each of those things at me during the rest of the day.

I felt like the most pampered female in Tolerance when he tucked me into bed after a fantastic steak dinner. Cuddled in his arms, I should have fallen right asleep. Instead, my eyes stayed open, aimed at a dark wall I couldn't see.

"Sleep, Shelby," Vorx said softly behind me.

"I'm not sure I can. We both know Turik wanted to be home by dark and only added dawn so I wouldn't worry. Do you think something happened?"

Vorx grunted and continued playing with my hair.

"He will be home by dawn," he said after a few heartbeats.

Doubt ate at me.

CHAPTER TWENTY

Dreams of running in fear filled my restless slumber, and the slight dip of the mattress beside me was enough to pull me free. Groggily, I opened my eyes to see Turik.

"You're home," I whispered a moment before wrapping my arms around him.

Any relief I felt dissipated at the shock of touching cold skin.

"You're never cold. What's wrong?" I asked, pulling back.

He chuckled, his eyes dancing with humor, and rolled so I lay on top of him.

"Everything is right. I took a cold shower, hoping you might want to warm me."

His hand smoothed down my back in a slow stroke that tempted me to give him what he wanted. First, there was something I needed, though.

"I want to know what happened. What took so long? Was it Nat? Was anyone hurt?"

Turik cupped my face and started peppering a thousand little kisses there, slowly melting away the fear that had solidified within me while he was gone. In its place, a warmth bloomed. Turik was home, and he wasn't hurt. Far from it. Based on the hard length pressing into my thigh, he felt more than fine. He wasn't even cold anymore.

A slow smile tugged at my lips.

"I think I'd like to turn the tables."

"There are no tables in here," he said, pulling back with a slight frown.

I closed the distance between us and tested the smooth texture of his lips while his hands moved slightly on my back. Encouraged, I opened my mouth and licked the curve of his lower lip.

A growl rumbled out of him a moment before he took control. With a feral hunger that stole my breath, his lips claimed mine. The first stroke of his tongue erased my reality and created a new one where only he and I existed.

He consumed me. Controlled me. But in ways that made me feel treasured and desperately needed.

Tearing my mouth from his, I panted for air, only to have it taken again when he nibbled along my jaw to my collarbone. Hot need burned its way through my center.

Desperate for more contact, I straddled his hips. Another growl rumbled through him, and he immediately arched against my core. I gasped and ground down on his hard length. His hands gripped my ass, keeping the pressure firm. Bolts of pleasure ran through me, building my need for more.

More contact. More skin on skin.

Leaning back, I tore my shirt over my head and watched the way Turik's pupils rounded at the sight of my bare breasts.

Movement to my left called attention to the fact we weren't alone.

My startled gaze slid to Vorx as he propped himself up on his elbow.

"You are perfect, Shelby."

"She is," Turik agreed.

Vorx leaned forward and caught my nipple in his mouth, flicking it with his tongue before sucking it gently. It sent another confusing bolt to my core, and I rubbed against Turik's hard length. He grunted and arched into me.

Feeling the first stirrings of panic, my gaze darted between the pair.

Vorx released me, placed a gentle kiss on my upper breast, and fluidly rose from the bed.

"I'll make us breakfast while you welcome Turik home."

He left the room without a backward glance, and I bit my lower lip in worry. They'd watched each other make out with me once before, but this had been different. Vorx had participated, and I hadn't been ready for it. I wasn't up for a threesome. I wasn't even ready for a full twosome. Yet the idea that I'd done something to give him the impression I'd rejected him tore at me.

"I didn't mean to…I didn't know…" I wasn't sure what to say because I wasn't sure what had just happened.

"No," Turik said, running his thumb over the lip I was nibbling. "There's no need for this."

"Is Vorx mad?" I asked, looking down at him.

"With you? About this?" He ran his hands up my bare sides and palmed my breasts. "Never."

I was in an emotional blender, feeling so much that I wasn't sure what I felt.

"I don't know what to do," I whispered.

"Do what makes you happy, Shelby. I look at you and see

hope and goodness. Time and hardships will never dull your beauty here." He set a hand over my heart. "I will embrace each day you choose to stay here and each moment you share with me."

And that was the problem, wasn't it? I wanted to share moments with him. With both of them.

He partially sat up and lightly kissed my lips, letting me choose if it was a goodbye or hello. Saying goodbye was impossible, though, so I opened my mouth and greeted him the way I wanted to. The way that made me happy.

His tongue boldly stroked against mine, and his hands tightened on my hips. I ground myself against him, loving the friction and wanting more but too afraid to take that next leap.

We broke apart, and he kissed his way down to my breasts, taking the one that Vorx had kissed into his mouth. It felt so dirty and wrong, yet so right, that he was loving that spot, too. Heat flooded me, and I gripped his hair. When he broke away to kiss the other side, I made a small sound of disappointment. He simply chuckled and gave the other breast the same attention as the first, driving me wild with need.

I felt so empty. So desperate to be filled.

"Please, Turik," I panted.

"Tell me what you need," he said.

"You. More."

He turned us, pressing me into the bed. My underwear vanished as he kissed a trail down from my breasts. When he reached the apex of my thighs, he pulled back and looked at me.

"You are as pretty here as Vorx said," he murmured before lightly placing a kiss on my folds. "I like the way you smell. Do you think you taste as good?"

151

He didn't give me a chance to answer before he licked me with the flat of his tongue from core to clit. A mewling cry escaped me, and I clutched the sheets.

"You taste better," he said, as if I'd asked for the verdict. Then he began licking me in a frenzy.

The orgasm ripped through me in seconds, and I held him in place while I rode his tongue. He chuckled and gently sucked my sensitive nub until the last wave of pleasure receded. Then he switched to leisurely thrusting his tongue inside of me for several long minutes while I simply lay there, waiting for my pulse to return to normal.

"I like how you welcome me home," he said, finally lifting his head to press a kiss to my inner thigh. "I will need to leave again soon."

"I'd rather you stay. I didn't sleep well without you here."

He grunted, his fingers lightly stroking the insides of my legs.

After a long minute of silence, I lifted my head to look at him and found him gazing at my center. An embarrassed flush crept into my cheeks, but the embarrassment fled when he reverently kissed my mound.

"Thank you for letting me see and taste your pussy, Shelby," he said, meeting my gaze.

"I'm pretty sure I'm supposed to be thanking you," I managed. "That was amazing."

Without looking away, he lightly kissed my clit. My hips jerked, and he glanced at me.

"Does that mean I can lick you some more?"

"I think I'm a little too sensitive for more right now. Why don't we shower together while you tell me what happened?"

He had me up in his arms so fast that I whipped my arms

around his neck and squealed a little. Then he was out the door, moving with enough speed through the house that there was a slight breeze on my bare ass.

"I can walk, Turik," I said. But he was already entering the master bathroom.

"I know you can," he said, putting me down. "But I could get us here faster."

He stripped in seconds, and my gaze locked on his engorged shaft while he turned on the shower. Unable to resist, I reached out and wrapped my hand around his length.

He straightened with a groan and set his hands on my shoulders, giving me free rein.

"Start talking," I encouraged while I stroked my hands up and down his length. "Why didn't you come home last night?"

"Home," he practically purred. "Yes."

"Focus, Turik. Why didn't you come back sooner? What happened?"

"We returned to the place where the shots had been fired and tracked the humans to a house. It was dark and quiet, but we could hear them move inside like they were hiding. We knew they had guns, so we waited for them to come out, but it took a long time."

He steered us into the shower and backed me into the water. Like the day before, he carefully wet my hair and started shampooing my scalp. It felt so good I almost forgot what I was doing. When I realized I was just standing there, I gave him a light squeeze. He hissed out a breath in appreciation.

"And?" I asked, picking up the conversation and the movement of my hand as he soaped me. "Were they the exiled men?"

"Yes. But only two. We moved them farther away. It will take them many days to return if they know how."

He rinsed my hair and started soaping my breasts, playing with them more than washing them. I loved it and focused my energy on discovering what types of touches drove him crazy. He absolutely loved when I stroked him and fondled his balls. I was about to bend down and add my mouth to the mix when he firmly gripped my shoulders.

"I will release if you keep doing this."

"That's kind of the point." I circled my fingers around his scrotum and rubbed a digit along the skin underneath.

He made a strangled sound a second before his cock jumped in my hand, and he painted my stomach with his release. Pressing his lips to my head and holding me close, he continued to thrust into my hand. He was breathing hard when he finished and tipped my face back to pepper it with kisses again. I basked in his attention and praise.

"Your soft hands know all the right places. You have my consent to touch me whenever you want; I don't need to be awake."

I grinned and started washing both of our mid-sections.

"I'll keep that in mind."

He rubbed some conditioner into my hair, playing with the strands. It was then that I realized the braids he'd put in my hair the day before were gone. With a fair amount of guilt, I recalled Vorx playing with them last night.

"Would you mind if I finish up alone?" I asked.

He brushed his lips lightly against mine.

"Enjoy your shower. I will wait for you in the kitchen."

He left, boldly and beautifully naked. I watched him go without any regret over what we'd shared but a little worried that I'd upset Vorx, no matter what Turik said. Having them both say they only wanted me to be happy was one thing. Watching me do that was another. Yet, that's exactly what they seemed to like to do.

I nibbled on my bottom lip and finished up in the bathroom. It wasn't until I was ready to leave that I realized no one had dropped off any clean clothes for me.

Smiling a little, I wrapped a towel around my torso and left the bathroom.

The soft murmur of their voices drifted to me before I reached them.

"She isn't afraid to touch us. I like that," Turik said.

"Me too," Vorx said. "And I like that she isn't afraid of our touch. Did she let you bathe her breasts like she let me yesterday?"

My steps slowed as I listened.

"Yes. She does like it. Her pulse jumped, but I think she reacted more strongly this morning when you put your mouth on one."

Vorx grunted. "She seemed to like your mouth on her pussy even better. Those were the best noises she's made yet."

"Her pussy tastes very good. I'm hungry for more just thinking about it. We will make her happy."

An ache started in my chest.

"Yes. She needs both of us," Vorx said.

"She doesn't see it yet, but she will," Turik agreed.

CHAPTER TWENTY-ONE

I wasn't exactly sure how to process what I'd overheard. That they were completely fine with the way things were going was clear. But they'd sounded like they were talking long-term. Both of them. With me.

Why were my insides doing all kinds of somersaults at the idea of that? Of a forever home with Turik *and* Vorx? I didn't want long-term. I just wanted to live one day at a time.

Liar, that inner voice mocked. It was far easier to lie to myself, though, than to hope for impossible things. Until they found Nat and "relocated" him, living day by day was the only smart option.

Smart or the safer option for your heart? my mind whispered.

I turned around and retreated to the bedroom to dig out some clothes. There was no point in dwelling on what might be; I needed to focus on the present.

Both fey turned to look at me when I stepped into the kitchen a few minutes later.

"Aren't either of you eating?" I asked when I saw only one cereal bowl.

"No," Vorx said. "The cereal is yours and not something we enjoy. Come. Sit."

He gestured to the chair next to Turik, and feeling awkward as hell, I took the seat.

"I can make you guys some of that meat gravy you liked and skip the biscuits."

Vorx poured the same kind of cereal I'd had the day before into the bowl and added milk.

"We already ate some of the canned meat," Turik said.

Feeling very watched, I slowly took a bite of cereal. It was just as good as the first time, and I forgot about my audience and enjoyed the food. When I sat back with a sigh, Vorx reached for the box.

"More?"

"No, thank you. Maybe tomorrow we could eat together so it's less weird, though?"

They both grunted.

"What are the plans for today?" I asked, glancing from Vorx to Turik. "Are you tired after staying up all night? Do you need sleep?"

"I'm not tired," Turik said. "What would you like to do?"

That two of the exiles had been so close to us had my thoughts turning from fishing to activities the three of us could do in Tolerance. Based on my conversation with Mya, the other women were trying to find ways to keep busy on a permanent basis. If I wanted to integrate with the community, I'd eventually need to talk to the other women. Just not yet.

"Let's stay in and watch movies for a bit. Maybe after lunch, we can walk around town and see if anyone needs help with anything."

I tried to take my bowl to the sink, but Turik beat me to it, and Vorx thwarted any attempt to wrestle the dish away from Turik when he swept me off my feet and deposited me on the couch.

"I can wash my own dishes."

Turik glanced back at me. "I can wash them too."

"I already know I want to stay. You don't need to keep spoiling me."

Vorx smirked and lifted my legs, moving me sideways as he sat to hold them captive. Not that I was struggling. He was just as good at foot rubs as Turik, and I made a soft sound of appreciation when he worked over my arch with his thumb.

"Fine. You've made your point. I'm addicted to your version of spoiling. But just remember this when I turn into a needy monster in a few months. You created me."

After Turik put away the dishes, he picked out a movie and joined us on the couch. With my head in one lap and my feet in the other, I settled in for some wholesome cartoon time.

Since the quakes released the hellhounds, there hadn't been time for idle TV watching. But even before that, I would have never dreamed of touching the remote, never mind turning on a cartoon for entertainment.

Vorx's chuckle at something on the screen had me smiling in his direction. He noticed and gave my ankle an extra little squeeze. There wasn't anything sexual behind it, but his touch, in addition to the glinting humor, equaled a panty-melting moment.

Turik's fingers toyed with my hair, adding to the explosion of sensations. And I loved it. Being touched by both of them.

While they kept it strictly non-sexual, my brain went the opposite direction, recalling the way Turik had kissed me and touched me this morning and the way I'd made him lose control. I glanced at Vorx, his calm expression while he watched TV, and thought of how much I wanted him to lose control, too.

I shifted my foot over, "accidentally" rubbing against the semi-hard length in his pants. His gaze immediately snapped to mine, but I was carefully staring at the TV. Thankfully, there was a cute part to explain my sudden smile. His fingers twitched on my ankle before he resumed watching the movie.

Anticipation built inside of me as I waited a few minutes before doing it again. He was no longer semi-hard but full-on "cut glass with it" hard. His gaze whipped to mine again. Once more, I remained focused on the TV.

"Do you feel safe here, Shelby?" Vorx asked, surprising me.

"Yes. Why?"

One minute, he was sitting with my legs on his lap, and the next, I was up in his arms.

"Don't make her pussy sore," Turik warned as Vorx started walking away with me. "Ghua said that three pussy lickings a day is a safe number."

"Wait, what?" I glanced at Turik over Vorx's shoulder, and Turik grinned wolfishly at me.

"Touch that spot on Vorx, too," he called before Vorx turned the corner into his room.

A second later, I lay on the bed we shared at night. Vorx reached for my waistband, tugging down my leggings to get to what he wanted. He didn't even have the patience to remove them. He stopped when they were around my ankles then lifted my legs, looping them around his shoulders.

"This," Vorx said, staring at me for a moment. "Turik was right. You smell good."

He kissed my thigh and looked up at me. The intensity of his gaze stole my breath.

"With Turik, or with me, you always have a choice. Do you understand?"

The hunger in his eyes contrasted with the patience and understanding behind his words. Yet, I knew without a doubt that he would hold true to what he said. Whatever I did with either Vorx or Turik would be my choice.

"Neither of you are Nat. I understand."

Holding my gaze, he lifted my hips like bringing a feast to his mouth. My breath caught as his exhale washed over my folds, and I waited for that first powerful slide of his tongue. At the last second, he ducked his head and nipped the tender underside of my cheek.

A little 'eep' escaped me.

"Did I hurt you?"

I shook my head, and the next bite elicited a completely different reaction. It sent signals straight to my core. My fingers twitched with the need to grab him by the ears and tug him to where I wanted him. He knew what his little love bites were doing to me, too, based on his knowing smirk.

"Is this payback for teasing you?" I asked.

"Not yet. I've been wanting to do this since Turik gave you the yellow shirt and the string underwear that showed me this beautiful backside."

I put my hands behind my head like they'd done when I was sleeping restlessly between the two of them. Vorx flashed a quick grin at me and dipped his head for the final time. He kissed me tenderly then lightly used his teeth on that spot before moving on. Kiss and nip. Kiss and nip. Every press of his lips built the anticipation for the feel of his teeth scraping my skin and the jolts of pleasure that teasing hint of barely contained passion sent to my core.

My backside tingled by the time he covered every inch.

"Are you ready to scream for me, my Shelby?"

That kind of question would have terrified me a week ago. Today, it filled me with hot desire, and I lifted my hips from his palms.

He grunted and leaned forward to tease his tongue along my folds. Where Turik used bold strokes, Vorx kept his touch light and brief. And he was driving me nuts. Soon I was shifting my hips to chase after him. He chuckled and kept avoiding the spot I desperately needed him to tongue.

"Please, Vorx," I begged. "Just lick me already."

"No."

He stopped licking entirely and went back to kissing and nibbling on my backside. The need built higher, and I squirmed in his palms before hooking my knees over his shoulders. It gave me more leverage to move to meet him, not that he gave in.

My pulse pounded in my ears, and need clawed at me. One lick. That would be all that I needed.

I gave up my death grip on the sheets and grabbed for his head. My right hand tangled in his hair, and the left caught his ear. He grunted and thrust his tongue deep inside of me.

A mangled moan tore from my throat, and I bucked against him. It felt amazing, but I needed more. I was so close.

"Please," I begged.

He thrust his tongue a few more times then withdrew, placing a single kiss directly on my clit.

My eyes went wide with understanding a second before his teeth closed over the sensitive nub.

The scream he ripped from me echoed in the room as I convulsed under his flicking tongue. I didn't move. I couldn't.

The light hold of his teeth kept me perfectly still as my world shattered into a million blissful pieces. Wave after wave of pleasure coursed through me, causing my channel to clench around nothing.

After the last one receded, Vorx finally gave me the long, slow licks I'd craved in the beginning.

"She tastes better than I imagined."

For a moment, I thought he was talking to himself.

"I wish pussies weren't so easily chafed by our tongues," Turik said. "I could lick her all day."

Frowning, I lifted my head to look down at Vorx, still sprawled between my legs, and Turik leaning in the doorway. Turik met my gaze and grinned at me.

"I didn't think Vorx would make you scream like he said. I will make you scream even louder next time."

My head flopped back onto the mattress. It was a very good thing they liked carrying me because I wasn't sure I would be able to walk if they kept this up.

"Taste her inside again," Turik instructed. "She's sweeter after she orgasms."

Vorx's tongue slipped inside of me again, and I happily closed my eyes.

CHAPTER TWENTY-TWO

AFTER ANOTHER SHOWER—ALONE AT VORX'S INSISTENCE— I returned to the living and the movie Turik had kindly paused for us. Once again taking my place between the pair, we snuggled on the couch until it was time for an early lunch.

Turik insisted on cooking while Vorx and I sat at the island and watched.

"What do you want to do after lunch?" I asked.

"I can shower with you again," Turik said. "I like the way your hands feel around my cock."

My gaze slid to Vorx. "How come you didn't want to try out my hands?"

"I am waiting and learning from Turik's mistakes."

Turik made a scoffing sound. "I do not make mistakes."

Vorx smirked at me before addressing Turik.

"I wouldn't give her my tongue until she begged for it, and she screamed her release. I won't give her my cock until she's weeping my name."

I stared at him, already imagining how much trouble I had headed my way.

"You gave her your cock too soon," he continued. "She will never beg for it now."

Turik didn't get angry; he simply turned to contemplate me.

"Vorx is right. I gave you my cock too soon." He sighed. "I will make you beg for it later tonight. After lunch, we will walk around town before you are too sore." He looked at Vorx. "How many times was Ghua able to pleasure Eden before she needed ice?"

"Whoa. Hold up. That does not sound fun."

Both fey blinked at me.

"I don't want to be so sore I can't walk. Don't get me wrong —the oral was great. But I'm not into sex that hurts."

A slow smile bloomed on Vorx's face, and in his expression, I could read what he was thinking.

"Those love-bites don't count. You were being gentle and didn't hurt me."

"And they led to pleasure that made you scream. Ghua makes Eden scream like that every time. It does not matter if he uses his mouth, fingers, or cock. He discovers what she needs and gives her everything. That's why Eden agrees to more pleasure even when she's sore and sits on ice when she's done."

I leaned back in my chair, a little in awe of Eden while also wondering how she felt about her sex life being common knowledge.

"I'm not even sure I'm ready for sex yet."

Both guys grunted noncommittally, and Vorx distracted me by placing a ham and cheese sandwich with mayo, pickles, and mustard in front of me.

"Wow. That's, um, a lot of flavors packed in there," I said, looking at all the pickles.

"It is one of Angel's favorite lunches," Turik said.

"Angel. The pregnant one?"

He nodded, and I inwardly cringed as I took my first bite under their watchful gazes. The saltiness in combination with the tang hit my tastebuds in the best way.

"This is way better than I thought it would be," I admitted. I glanced at both of them and realized they'd done it again.

"Can we please eat a meal at the same time?"

Turik and Vorx shared a look that I couldn't immediately decipher.

"The bread is for you," Turik said.

I connected the dots and shook my head at them.

"We don't need to eat the same thing. I get that you don't like bread and prefer meat. That's fine. I just want us to eat together. Like a…I don't know. A family." The last word took some work to get out, but I managed and hurried to press on. "Nat always ate first, like it was some kind of show of dominance. I don't want to eat first. I don't want anyone feeling like they're better than anyone else. Does that make sense?"

Turik plucked me off my stool, sat me in his lap, and hugged me hard.

"Vorx and I do not believe we are better than the other. We like to challenge one another because it makes us both better."

I looked up at Turik's earnest expression and slowly shook my head.

"You are so sweet to clarify that. Thank you. But I was truly just talking about eating."

"We will eat dinner together tonight."

I smiled and leaned forward to kiss his cheek. He let me slide off his lap and take my seat.

"Do I get no kiss?" Vorx asked.

"I don't know. Maybe I'm going to withhold those from you

so you want them more." I arched a brow at him. "How does that feel?"

The sexy smirk he shot my way was downright dangerous.

"It will feel very good when you finally allow me to taste your lips."

I muttered "ridiculous" under my breath and hurried to eat my sandwich.

The silence gave my headspace too much breathing room, though. Thoughts started popping in. Thoughts of how quickly my life had changed. How much I liked living in this house. Then questions about the future. And those always circled back to what I was doing and what I'd overheard earlier.

My life with Nat had been so messed up. Wasn't I headed down another messed-up road by making out with two men on the same day? Two, I might add, who lived together in the same house and seemed completely fine with the fact that I needed them both? Need. That should have been too strong for the situation. Or, at least, too soon for it. But it wasn't. I needed them in so many small ways and a few big ones, too.

Back in the bedroom, just before Vorx finally gave me the orgasm of a lifetime, I'd been thinking about how empty I felt and how I'd wanted to feel full and loved. If Vorx had stripped down then, I would have jumped on him faster than a squirrel on a pecan tree in fall. What about Turik, then?

I realized I'd stopped eating, and my gaze was bouncing between the two fey in question, who were watching me in return.

Slowly, I set down my sandwich.

"I need help understanding your expectations so I can manage my own," I said. "Because I'm a little messy here right now." I tapped my head. "You both want to have sex with me, right?"

They each nodded.

"And having sex with one of you doesn't mean I choose that one. I get to keep both of you until you don't want to be kept, right?"

"You will keep both of us," Vorx said.

"Both of us want to be kept by you forever," Turik added.

"Okay. Sure. But what about babies? I'm not sure I want to have those when I can't even take care of myself."

"That is why you have two of us," Vorx said.

"We'll take care of you and any babies we someday have," Turik said.

I let that image settle in my head for a moment. Me and two doting fey. Two dads to protect any kids we might have. The idea wasn't horrible. Not at all.

"How do you think people are going to react to the three of us having that type of relationship? One woman with two fey husbands?"

Turik's expression took on a cat that ate the canary gleam.

"Two husbands sounds very good."

"I don't think you're focusing on the question. What happens if I have sex with both of you going forward? Polyamorous relationships aren't socially acceptable by most United States citizens. The likelihood of me being shunned by the other humans is high, and I don't want to get kicked out again.

"I like living here with both of you. I love the way you're spoiling me. Your goal was to make me feel safe and not want to leave. Well, I do feel safe, and I really don't want to leave.

But I think that's exactly what I'll be forced to do if I have sex with both of you.

"And it's messing with my head because I don't simply want to have my cake and eat it too. I want a damn bucket of ice cream with it."

Their slightly troubled expressions shifted to pure confusion.

"I can make a lemon cake," Turik said, standing. "But we don't have any ice cream."

"I can leave and—"

"That's not what I meant," I said, cutting off Vorx and stopping both of them. "It means that I want to be able to have this house, the feeling of safety, and both of you in my life. But right now, it feels like I have to choose between having this home and having the two of you."

Turik and Vorx shared a long look. Finally, Turik met my gaze.

"You can have both. We will tell our brothers that humans don't believe in two husbands, and they will not tell the humans."

"Do you honestly think that Ghua, who is telling you every detail about his sex life with Eden, will keep a secret from her?"

"If telling her means we would need to find a home away from our brothers, yes."

I understood then what Vorx and Turik were saying. It wasn't a matter of choosing. The choice was already made. We were a package deal in their heads. If I was shunned, we would all be shunned. And knowing that made the situation that much harder.

"I think I need some fresh air," I said, pushing my plate away.

Ten minutes later, I was using my own two feet to make my way to the place where some of the Tolerance women liked to meet up. Turik explained that it was a training area with a large plastic target for archery and dummies for stabbing. But they both lit up when they mentioned the grass ring where the women "struggle with one another."

"They used to start earlier, but Angel likes to sleep longer now, and the others like when Angel yells at them."

They were painting a weird picture that didn't come close to reaching the appropriate level for what I saw when I arrived. The large plastic target was actually a pile of melted sex toys. Angel, the only visibly pregnant woman in attendance, wasn't yelling at the other women. She was down on her knees, hitting the ground as she counted out a pin. The other non-wrestling participants were looking on with amusement while holding bows.

"Three," Angel yelled. "Hannah is the winner of this round. Stand up and take it like a woman, Eden. Hannah's choice."

Hannah extended her hand to the scowling Eden and helped her off the ground.

"Just remember, I was good to you on the last one," Eden said.

Hannah's smile was pure radiance.

"How can I forget? Your dare earned me a bareback spanking that made it hard to sit for lunch."

"Don't even pretend that it wasn't worth it," Angel said, struggling to her feet with the help of a fey. "According to what I heard, you were having a grand old time until Merdon broke free of the handcuffs."

Hannah's smile softened and turned secretive.

"So worth it. Which is why I'm going to return the favor. So what's it going to be? Truth or Dare?"

Eden's panicked gaze swept over the bystanders and landed on me.

"Look! The new girl is here. Hi, Shelby. Come on over and meet everyone."

She marched over to hook her arm through mine and dragged me toward her circle of friends.

"This is Hannah." She pointed to the match-winner with the curly blonde hair. "And Angel." She indicated the pregnant lady. "And Brenna and Tasha." The two with the bows.

"Hi," I said, trying for friendly but feeling inept.

"So what do you think of feight club? Stands for fey fight club. Although, come to think of it, that name doesn't make much sense when it's all human women in the club. Want to join? We have archery and knifing dummies and—"

"Cut the crap, Eden," Hannah said. "Truth or Dare, or I pick for you."

"Fine. Dare."

"I have a feeling I'm going to need to cover my ears for this," Tasha said, pivoting and walking away.

Angel sniggered, and Hannah crossed her arms while smirking at Eden.

"Dare it is," the curly blonde almost purred. "I heard Ghua stumbled upon an adult toy store a few days ago."

"You wouldn't," Eden whispered, her eyes going wide.

CHAPTER TWENTY-THREE

"I THINK THAT'S MY CUE TO SAY TODAY'S SESSION IS DONE," Brenna said, already turning away from the group. "See you ladies tomorrow."

Angel noticed my confusion and moved closer to my side while Eden stared imploringly at Hannah.

"What we have here," Angel stage-whispered, "is a bet with benefits. Eden's man, Ghua, loves anything to do with sex, and Hannah's trying to help Eden broaden her horizons."

"I think it's time," Hannah said with a smirk.

"I'm going to need to go back to being twelve for a year," Eden said.

"If you can hold out that long after you explain every item in that store to him."

Eden paled.

"No," she whispered. "Not that. Mya doesn't want the fey corrupted."

"Pfft," Angel said. "They're thousands of years old and just discovered females. There's nothing in that store that they're not already thinking about."

Eden shot Hannah a pleading look. "Can I change my answer to Truth?"

"Nope. That ship's sailed," Hannah said.

Eden turned to me and made a face. "Wrestling with Hannah is dangerous, especially when there's betting involved. Definitely start with archery. Much safer."

I glanced at Brenna, the woman still holding the bow, then the target.

"With a target made of dildos, anal beads, and a fisting hand, I don't think there will be much left at the adult toy store to discover."

The soft murmur of nearby fey conversation fell quiet, and all three women stared at me. Angel started howling with laughter about two seconds later. Eden flushed a deep red, and Hannah grinned widely at me.

"You would be correct there, Shelby. But those are the previously owned sex toys that Ghua collected before he met Eden. She and Mya burned them. You know, for sanitary purposes," Hannah said. "The toy store would have brand new toys that females here could use with their fey if they wanted to."

"You have a mean streak a mile wide," Eden said.

"She does," Angel agreed. "But she's also the sweetest person you know right now. She's helping rip off the bandage. Once it's gone, you'll be less worried about what Ghua's thinking at any given moment."

"Bring me back an anal plug," Hannah said. "Maybe Merdon will think twice about spanking me when I start moaning."

"Look at their wonderful faces," Angel said before laughing so hard she started crying.

I glanced at the fey. Their expressions ranged from confused to stunned.

Eden's fey came up behind her and set his hands on her shoulders.

"How much of that did you understand?" she asked without looking at him.

"I'm not sure. How much did you want me to understand?"

Her face flushed scarlet while Hannah patted Ghua on the shoulder.

"You're a perfect gentleman, Ghua. Make sure she explains each item to you. A bet's a bet. Let me know how it goes when you drop off my gift."

He picked up the flaming Eden without another word and started jogging away. At least twenty other fey swarmed from the shadows to join them.

"Are they going on a supply run at the sex toy store?" I asked just to make sure I wasn't misunderstanding the conversation.

"They sure are," Hannah said. "Need anything?"

I glanced at Vorx and Turik, who were standing not far away with a rather stoic-looking fey a few inches taller than they were.

"No. I think I'm good for now."

"Which one were you looking at?" Angel asked, wiping her eyes. "I couldn't tell."

"I'm living with both of them," I said vaguely.

"Ooh. Two for the price of one. Lucky girl. Terri's living the sweet life too."

"Heard Groth gave her a boob rub while Azio watched," Hannah said. "Fey willing to share are rare."

"The sweet things wouldn't need to share if there were more

willing women." Angel reached out and gave my arm a squeeze. "Good on you if you can handle two. They deserve every bit of happiness they can wrangle."

It was my turn to stare at the pair.

"I can't decide if I'm being pranked or encouraged."

"Neither," Angel said firmly. "We're letting you know we don't judge here."

"Um. Okay. Thanks, I think."

I glanced at Vorx and Turik again. Vorx was smirking, and Turik was giving me a heated look. When I faced Hannah and Angel again, both women were grinning at me.

"Oh, yeah, you're going to have your hands full. You might want to have your fey raid the storage shed for extra ice cube trays. Heard that's what Ghua did for Eden."

"About that. Does she know her sex life is common knowledge?"

"Oh, yeah," Hannah said with a laugh.

"Don't worry," Angel said. "Hers isn't the only one. They're learning that a bit of rough play can turn a girl on, thanks to Hannah, and that doggie-style is more enjoyable to some women, thanks to me, and about periods, and so much more from us all. They take it in, compare notes, and use the information to be the best, most-loving men for their women. All we need to do is love them back with equal intensity, and they're in heaven. Right, babe?" She shifted her gaze to the fey, who moved to stand next to her.

"Exactly," he said, carefully picking her up.

She grinned at me.

"Yesterday, Shax picked me up too quickly, and I peed a little. He learned. Now they all know. Pregnant bladders aren't the strongest."

He grunted.

"Onward, my mighty steed."

Hannah snorted. "Now he's going to be thinking about you riding him."

"I know," Angel said with a wicked smile as she toyed with his ear. "And he's going to want to run home with me but won't because it makes me queasy."

Shax made a growly noise and kissed her hard.

"Later, girls!" she called breathlessly as he strode away with her. "Tell Emily I'm around if she needs me."

Hannah lifted a hand in farewell then stuck her hands in her jacket pockets and considered me.

"If you want to join feight club, try to be here about an hour after sunrise. I promise not to take it too easy on you."

"I think I'll pass on feight club." I'd had enough of being tossed around to last me a lifetime. "But thanks for the invite."

She gave me a puzzled look. "So what brought you out here today?"

"I was hoping to meet some of the other women. Gauge how welcome I am here."

"You are welcome, Shelby," Turik said firmly behind me.

"I was kicked out of Tenacity for my part in what happened to Adam and June," I said, just to put it all out there in the open.

"No, you kicked yourself out because you were too afraid to leave your shitty ex. No one here has any problem with you, except for maybe you. I'm not judging. I was so deep in self-hate, I couldn't see it. Let go of the past and embrace the present for all it's worth. There's no guarantee it'll last long."

"Hannah," one of the fey said sharply.

"Shut it, Merdon. I'm trying to be encouraging."

"I appreciate the advice. And I know this isn't likely to last long. My ex will try to make sure of that."

"I heard. Two down and ten more to go, right? The fey will find him and relocate him like they did with the other men. He's nothing compared to the other shit we're dealing with. I'm more worried about the hellhounds coming out during the day. That shit isn't okay."

Merdon closed the distance between them in a blink and unceremoniously tossed her over his shoulder, ignoring her indignant squeal.

"You have nothing to worry about, Shelby," he said. "Vorx and Turik will keep human men, infected, and hellhounds from you. All females are safe here."

"Tell that to the ones who died during the breach," Hannah said, arching up to look back at him. "Pretending a threat isn't there isn't safety; it's ignorant. And I refuse to be that ignorant again. I'd rather be prepared."

"Don't worry. I will prepare you." He smoothed a hand over her backside, and she grinned at me.

"Give us a thirty-minute head start then come by to talk to Emily. She'll show you around and introduce you to everyone."

Merdon jogged away, leaving me with Vorx and Turik and a few curious fey onlookers.

"I have to say that didn't go like I'd imagined it would."

"Is that bad?" Turik asked.

"I'm not sure yet," I said honestly. "So, what do we want to do for thirty minutes?"

CHAPTER TWENTY-FOUR

THEY SHOWED ME THE ANIMAL PENS, WHICH IMPRESSED THE HELL out of me. I could have stayed there and watched them for hours. As it was, we were later than Hannah suggested when we knocked on the door.

A young woman with light brown hair and soft brown eyes answered our knock and invited us in with a welcoming smile.

"I was so excited when Hannah mentioned you might stop over. I'm Emily. Welcome to Tolerance."

"Thank you."

"Hannah said you were interested in getting to know people here." She gestured for us to join her in the living room. "Rather than going house to house and hoping to catch people at a good time, I have a different idea. Tolerance needs to build up our skilled labor pool, so we're doing some workshops. Things like baking, sewing, knitting, weaving, gardening...you name it, we're trying to find people who have a natural affinity with it or people who already know how to do it and can teach it. We're going to meet up in the afternoons for a few hours, and

I'd like you to join in. It's a perfect way to meet everyone. What do you think?"

"It sounds interesting. Mya mentioned something about finding a profession when I met her."

"Great! I'll add you to the list. We're meeting here this afternoon with a few people from Tenacity who are interested."

Inside, I shriveled a little.

"I'm looking forward to finding a way to contribute. I really am. But I think it would be better, for now, if I sit out on the group meetings. June and Matt went through a lot of effort to clean out the bad apples—"

"You're not one of them," Emily said quickly, taking one of my hands in her own.

It was clear her heart was in the right place, but she wasn't thinking of the consequences.

"Everyone here has been very clear that they are okay with me living with Turik and Vorx. But that's because everyone here understands what happened that night. The people at Tenacity don't. What kind of message would it send them if a person publicly exiled for stealing is now living the good life with the fey?"

Emily made a pained face.

"You're right. I'll add that to my list of things to discuss with June when I see her this afternoon. We'll work on a way to clear your name there so everyone understands."

"How are things going over there?" I couldn't help asking.

"A little chaotic with people reorganizing who they want to live with, and a fair number are leaving to help Ryan with the new place. I think they've realized that they'll have more room and better protection if they jump on the mingled community bandwagon. Here, they'd need permission from the core group of women. There, it's still open for everyone."

A sick feeling settled into my stomach.

"I need permission to be here?"

Turik picked me up and sat me in his lap, wrapping me in one of his amazing hugs.

"You already have it," Emily said with humor lacing her words. "You had it before you even agreed to come home with Turik. If you haven't yet caught on, word spreads fast here. Tor knew Turik was going after you and let Drav know before you even left Tenacity. I'm glad you said yes, by the way. I wasn't sure I would be able to find a woman willing to take on two fey. I mean, they all treat each other like brothers, but these two troublemakers are tighter than usual. Thankfully, they're the only package deal I know of."

"Wait...so everyone here knows they both want to hook up with me?" I asked, stunned.

Emily sat back and gave me a sheepish smile.

"Yes, but it's not a big deal if you do or don't. The choice is yours. And they won't be upset if you choose one and not the other. The fey aren't petty like that."

Turik pressed a kiss to the top of my head.

"Shelby isn't ready to choose. She is still finding her happiness."

"Aww! Turik, that was the sweetest, most understanding thing to say." Emily shifted her gaze to me. "He really is the sweetest." Then Vorx. "You are too, Vorx. Just not with the words. You do sweet things, and that's just as important."

I watched Emily's face as she praised them. The people in Tenacity knew her as the fey cheerleader, and it fit.

"Where's your fey?" I asked.

"Like you, I'm not ready yet. I want to make sure Hannah's settled and happy and keep working on finding women for all the fey before grabbing one for myself. I know how distracting they can be."

There was a sudden thumping coming from upstairs, like someone hitting a wall.

"Is everything okay?" I asked when she cringed.

"Yeah. Sorry. Hannah came down to check if you were here but went back upstairs when you were late. Apparently, they started up again even though I know Merdon can hear we have company."

Vorx chuckled. "Hannah provoked him at practice."

"She always provokes him."

"Yes, but she asked Eden to bring back a sex toy that will make Hannah enjoy her spanking time."

Emily rubbed her face and shook her head. "On that note, I think I'm going to go visit Mary and James this afternoon."

We stood with her and went to the door.

"Don't be a stranger," Emily called as we left.

"Today just keeps getting weirder," I said to Vorx and Turik. "Would either of you mind if we just go home and hole up for a while?"

Neither objected, and we were again cuddled on the couch fifteen minutes later. Instead of laying across them, I sat between them, leaning my head on Turik while idly holding Vorx's hand and playing with his fingers.

One of them had picked a movie for us, but I wasn't watching. I was thinking of what I'd learned today. First, Turik and Vorx were both okay with sharing me. Second, all the fey seemed to have a sex addiction. Third, the females here were okay with all of it. And the most important thing—everyone here seemed to know that Vorx and Turik were a package deal for some lucky lady.

Releasing Vorx, I reached out for the remote and paused the movie.

"When you first walked in that door, you asked what I was doing here," I said, looking at Vorx. "If you two are so close, does that mean Turik didn't talk this over with you before bringing me home? Are you settling for me because I'm willing and here?"

"No, Shelby. I was there too. I saw how afraid you were as you knelt beside your husband for hours, and I saw the shame in your eyes when you left. But you never wavered, and you never looked back. I knew Turik would try to win you, but I didn't think you would leave your husband for us.

"When I saw you here, I needed to know why before I allowed myself to hope."

"And Emily thinks you don't have a sweet tongue."

He smirked at me. "Would you like me to remind you how sweet my tongue is?"

I rolled my eyes at him even as anticipation curled inside of me.

"What I'd like to understand is why the two of you are a package deal. Don't get me wrong; I like the attention I'm getting from both of you. But Emily's right that you're both equally amazing. If you've lived thousands of years, what's a few more months of patience to wait for a woman for each of you? Wouldn't you like to have some woman's undivided attention, too?"

Turik and Vorx did that shared look thing again.

"I'm serious. Why share?"

"In those thousands of years, we died many times," Turik

said. "We learned from each other, and as we got stronger, we died less. Until it was many, many years since our last death."

"Our world was dangerous," Vorx said. "But we learned how to survive it. Together."

"Then our dangers were unleashed on your world. A world filled with soft, beautiful females. Many died those first days. We see them every time we leave this place, and removing their heads brings us pain." Turik put a hand over his heart to show where he hurt. "But it reminds us what will happen if we cannot protect our females."

"We understand this world's dangers," Vorx said. "Eden almost died during the breach because Ghua was fighting too many infected alone. If Turik and I share a female, she will never be alone. We will fight together to protect you."

The level of safety they were offering spoke to me on a profound level. I wanted that—ultimate protection from Nat, the infected, and hellhounds. And their method worked. Look at what had happened at the house. Vorx had focused on fighting the hellhound, and Turik had run with me. Without their teamwork, what would have happened?

I swallowed hard and looked down at my hands, hoping I would never have to find out.

"Okay," I said finally. "I'll stop questioning if this is real. I'll stay. Forever. No changing your minds.

This is me accepting that you're both choosing me, and I'm choosing both of you."

They both made growling sounds of satisfaction. Turik picked up my hand and kissed the tip of each finger. Then Vorx stole that hand and lightly bit the pad of each finger. My stomach dipped, and a zing of pleasure lit through me.

"She likes biting," Vorx murmured.

"No, she doesn't," I said.

"Shh," Turik said, nuzzling my ear. "You do."

He proved it by lightly nibbling on my earlobe.

My pulse sped at the sensation, and my lips parted. Vorx chuckled, watching my reaction to Turik's attention. His calculated study made me nervous and a little needy.

"Let's go back to watching our movie, okay?"

Vorx turned on the show, but Turik didn't stop his slow assault on my ear. And I was enjoying it too much to turn away. Each scrape of his teeth added to the building pleasure, and I struggled to control my breathing. Slowly, he worked his way down along my jaw until he claimed my lips.

I groaned at the first touch of his tongue to mine and wrapped my arms around his neck as he lifted me to straddle his lap. Hands skimmed up my sides, fingers against bare skin. I shivered at the sensation and broke away from the kiss just long enough to lift my arms so Vorx could finish removing my shirt. Turik reached around to unhook my bra and free my breasts.

The satisfied sound he made and the way he gazed at my chest fed the flames inside of me. My core clenched around nothing as I waited for what he'd do next.

"Look at how perfect she is," he said.

I turned my head and found Vorx standing over us. Like Turik, he was watching me with a ravenous gaze.

"Do you still think you can make her scream louder?" Vorx asked.

Heat flooded my face, and I felt myself clench again.

Turik's mouth skimmed the underside of my breast in answer. His tongue followed. Then his teeth. Everything was light and teasing. Hinting at what he could do and feeding the fire within me until I blazed with desperation.

My hands fisted his hair. Little pleading sounds escaped me.

"Please, Turik. Just put your damn mouth on me already."

"It is on you," he said just before kissing the second breast without ever taking my nipple into his mouth.

"You know what I mean."

He chuckled and continued his slow assault. I turned my head, desperately seeking Vorx. He sat in a chair now and watched us with avid focus.

"Soon," he said.

A shiver ripped through me at the promise in that single word.

CHAPTER TWENTY-FIVE

"Take your clothes off, Shelby," Vorx said, not moving from his spot.

The heat in his gaze drew me away from Turik's love bites. Shaking with need, I stood and slowly lowered my pants over my hips. Then I turned so both had a decent view and continued down, bending at the waist until I had everything at my ankles.

A light bite on my lower back elicited another moan from me.

"So pretty," Vorx said, running his hand over the curve of my ass. "Back to Turik."

He turned me, and I saw Turik in the same spot but completely naked. His cock rose dark and hard between his slightly spread legs. I stared at his impressive size, already imagining how it would feel sliding inside of me.

"No sex," Turik said, breaking into my daydream. "We know you are not ready. We will hug some more."

Hug? Screw hugs. They couldn't start my engine like this and then tell me I couldn't race.

"Do I get a choice?" I asked.

"Always," Vorx answered. "If you're not ready for pussy-cock hugs, Turik will lick your pussy and drink your sweet release."

Another clench.

"No, I mean about sex. What if I want sex?"

"Not until you're ready to scream," he said against my ear.

I shivered again.

"I'm ready now." It was supposed to come out confidently strong, but the tightness in my throat strangled it to a whisper.

"Not yet. But you will be. Up, my pretty Shelby."

He picked me up, and Turik gripped my thighs to guide me over his knees and settle me onto his lap, a healthy distance away from his twitching length. Before I could complain, Turik leaned forward and licked the nipple of the breast he'd thoroughly teased.

I mewled and tipped toward him only to have him go to the other side and pick up where he'd left off. Need clawed at me. I wanted his mouth on my breast, sucking hard. Biting. Making me clench.

A gasp ripped out of me when I felt a hand stroke along the back of my thigh. When it reached the base of my ass, it slipped between my legs and lightly traced the length of my folds. Bracing my hands on Turik's shoulder, I spread myself wider over his lap to give Vorx better access.

Turik grunted in appreciation at having my breasts closer and massaged the one he wasn't methodically nibbling his way around.

The two sensations melded together—Turik teasing me with licks and kisses and bites closer to my nipples, and Vorx lightly touching between my legs, closer and closer to my clit.

The moment Turik's mouth finally closed over me, Vorx rubbed his fingers over my sweet spot. The orgasm, which had been hovering just out of reach, crashed through me, and I tipped my head back, releasing a low, almost pained wail. I rode it out on Vorx's fingertips, wishing for something far more substantial.

"Again," I panted when small aftershocks were dancing along my inner walls.

Vorx kissed the back of my neck then used his teeth there. I shivered.

"Three is enough for today," he said. "We'll pleasure you some more tomorrow."

I frowned at Turik, who had a view of my face.

"We don't want to hurt you, Shelby."

"Let me be the judge of when it's enough, then."

I lowered my hips, pressing my wet folds against his shaft. He hissed a breath and leaned his head back when I rocked against him. The feel of his engorged head sliding against my clit was almost too much. After three orgasms, it was plenty sensitive. But I was determined.

Shifting a little to the right for less direct contact, I continued rocking against him until his pupils were entirely blown. Only then did I lift my hips and grab his length to position it at my entrance. A second later, I was bent over the couch cushions with Turik thrusting against my folds.

"Not yet, my Shelby," he panted. "Trust us. Please."

I made an agitated sound and arched into his thrusts. Three orgasms should have been enough. But the ache inside of me demanded more attention than my tender clit begged for a break. I needed one of them inside of me. Filling me.

Turik's thrusts became erratic before I could make my

demands, and he moved from thrusting against my slick folds to thrusting between my cheeks. The contact of his hot length rubbing against my back entrance made me clench again.

He grunted and came in a torrent on my lower back.

"Ass-cock hugs might be better than pussy cock hugs," he panted. "I could feel her clenching back there."

"Did it hurt you, Shelby?" Vorx asked.

Keeping my heated face in the cushions, I shook my head.

Turik's weight left me, and a moment later, someone was cleaning off my back.

"Was the clenching because it felt good when he touched you here?"

A wet finger skimmed around places fingers didn't belong.

"I'm not ready for that," I said, straightening abruptly.

"Shh," Vorx said, wrapping me in a hug from behind. "I can hear your heart racing in fear. Turik and I won't force anything. You choose. We're only trying to understand."

I exhaled in relief and melted into his embrace.

"I don't know if I'll ever be ready for that," I said. "Okay?"

"Okay."

He picked me up and carried me to the bathroom. He didn't leave me to shower alone, but didn't start anything in there either. Rather, he tenderly washed me and helped me dress in the clothes Turik had slipped into the bathroom.

When we emerged, they hauled out the cookbooks they'd collected, and we poured through them together to come up with a dinner we would all enjoy. I'd never enjoyed spending hours in the kitchen, typically finding food prep a thankless chore. But I wasn't in it alone this time. They wanted to be there. We worked together. As a team. As equals.

Vorx chopped, Turik mixed, and I consulted the book and gathered ingredients. They teased each other and me while we worked. We laughed and had fun, and when everything was in the oven, we set the table together.

I stopped moving for a moment and just watched them.

My guys.

The evil fey who were the cause of all the world's troubles, according to Nat.

Vorx was giving Turik crap that his knife was crooked, and I grinned. This was the life I never knew I wanted. Vorx had seen the truth long before I had. I hadn't only been living a life filled with fear. I'd been lonely. Starved for affection and a comforting touch.

I would never starve for love again. I would never be lonely because one of them would always be with me. And I would always be safe.

I woke with a stretch and a smile. Today was a new day, and the orgasm limit was officially reset.

My hand snaked across the sheet and…touched nothing but more sheet. Cool sheet, in fact.

Frowning, I lifted my head and checked both sides of me, confirming what I'd suspected. My guys were gone.

"What the hell?" I muttered.

A chuckle drew my gaze to the doorway where Vorx leaned.

"Did you think we would stay in bed so you could torment us with your sweet ass-cock hugs?"

I scowled harder at his smirk.

"Up, woman." He straightened away from the door. "Hannah told you to meet her an hour after dawn, and you don't want to be late."

"I don't want to wrestle," I said, scrambling out of bed to chase after him.

"It's not wrestling," Turik said when I caught up to Vorx in the kitchen. "Vorx and I will do everything to ensure your safety, but you need to do your part, too. Hannah and Eden will show you how to avoid an infected bite. Brenna will teach you to use the bow, and we'll help you learn to use a knife."

"It's fighting. It's getting hit, and it'll hurt. Haven't I had enough of both?"

Vorx cupped my cheeks in his palms and kissed my forehead then my nose.

"Maybe you will save yourself with these skills. Maybe you will save one of us. Or, someday, a child. Aren't those skills worth learning for a chance to do all of that?"

I held his gaze for a long moment, hating that he was right and that I'd have to endure anything physical like that again.

"I don't want to do it," I whispered.

"I know," he said tenderly. "But you will. You're strong and have more courage than you know."

I closed my eyes, hating that he saw me that way because it meant I would need to live up to those expectations.

His lips gently brushed over mine, startling my eyes open.

"My sweet, pretty Shelby."

"Fine, but I better get all the pampering when I'm done."

He kissed my forehead again.

"You will. Go get dressed so we can eat breakfast together."

Withholding the face I wanted to make, I marched to the

master bedroom and pulled out some warm clothes. That was when I noticed Turik's things were missing.

"What's going on?" I called.

This time, Turik appeared in the doorway.

"Why are your clothes gone?" I demanded.

"To keep things equal, like you said, I asked our brothers to bring back one of the clean mattresses from the lake house. We all have our own rooms, but we can keep sleeping in Vorx's bed or here or wherever you want. It's up to you."

"What if I want to sleep alone?"

He flashed his teeth at me.

"You would toss and turn for a while and eventually call for us to join you. Do you want to try that tonight?"

"You're just as cocky as Vorx. How did I not see that until now?"

He chuckled before glancing around the room.

"Azio said that Terri likes their sex to be private from Groth." He shrugged lightly. "Your bruises are fading, and we wanted you to have private space for sex when you're ready."

I gave a relieved laugh.

"Well, that answers the one question I've been too chicken to ask. I thought you both wanted to have sex with me at the same time and was trying not to panic at the prospect. I wouldn't mind oral and vaginal, but anal is something I've never—"

"That's possible?" he asked.

Too late, I realized my mistake. Despite all the talk about anal beads and plugs and sex toys yesterday, the fey didn't know about any of it, which explained Eden's panic.

A flush consumed my face as I imagined all the information sharing that would take place today.

"I'd rather not talk about this anymore. In fact, can we pretend this conversation never happened? Please?"

He nodded slowly. "Of course."

I could see he wasn't forgetting the conversation, though. He was thinking about it so hard that I wasn't sure he could see me anymore.

CHAPTER TWENTY-SIX

I HURRIED FROM THE BEDROOM. WHEN I REACHED THE KITCHEN, Vorx gave me a slow, smirking smile that made my insides go crazy.

"You heard nothing."

"I heard everything, my Shelby."

"I'm not hungry. Can we just go now?"

Turik grunted behind me and plucked me off my feet.

"When are you going to give us your full trust? The thing we aren't talking about scared you. We can see that. Vorx likes to tease. The more you worry about this, the more he will tease. But he will never take what's not given. Neither of us will. Now eat."

He plunked me down in the chair and sat next to me. Vorx took the other side but kept sliding me glances while he ate his meat.

"There's no chance you're going to forget what you heard, is there?"

"Never," Vorx said. "I'm too curious and have so many questions."

"Well, don't look to me for answers. It's not my area of expertise."

He grunted and took another bite. I could feel him watching me as he chewed.

"What?" I asked finally.

"Are anal beads and fisting hands part of anal sex?"

"Absolutely no on the fists. Do you even see the size of your hands? That would kill me."

He paled. That large, scary-as-hell fey, who could kill dozens of infected and then a hellhound, paled at the thought of hurting me.

I immediately regretted my sharp tone.

"Vorx, I'm sorry. I didn't mean to say it like that. I would like to reiterate that I know next to nothing about the topic we're still not discussing. Who do you normally get your sex information from?"

"Ghua or Angel," Vorx said.

"Sometimes Mary, but James said we need to ask him the questions first before we ask Mary so he can make sure she doesn't get too overworked." Turik blinked at me. "We think he means her heart. Mya says that older people can have weaker hearts."

"You know what? I think James is your best option for this question." I'd met Angel and Ghua. Given Ghua's trip to the toy store yesterday, I could only imagine what kind of information he would come back with. A grandpa-type would probably tell my guys what they were asking about doing was considered rude by his generation, which would be just fine with me.

"And can we just focus on getting to know each other better and having normal sex for now? Normal sex can be very good."

They both grunted and resumed eating. Hoping the subject would never rear its head again, I dug into my cereal with a vengeance.

Fifteen minutes later, Brenna and Hannah welcomed me at the feight club area. My guys immediately moved off to talk in quiet tones with their guys.

"Want to get in on the betting?" Hannah asked.

"What are you betting on?" I asked.

"Whether Eden will show after yesterday's trip to the adult store," Brenna said. She looked at Hannah. "Mom nearly peed herself when I told her what you made her do this time. Then she told Uan he should have gone with." Brenna made a pained face. "Sometimes, I wish we weren't so open as a family."

Hannah laughed. "No, you don't. It would be even more painful for you now because the fey are extremely open. Look at those four whispering over there."

All four of our guys stopped talking and looked at us.

"That's right," Hannah said. "We know what you're talking about." She shook her head and rolled her eyes at me. "I didn't get what I wanted, but you can bet they pilfered toys, which are being hoarded somewhere for investigation and discussion. Merdon knows something, but he's not talking. We need Eden to tell us what happened."

Angel called out a hello, and we watched her sedate arrival.

"When is that kid going to come out already?" Hannah asked.

Angel shrugged. "Soon. We're guessing I'm somewhere in the final four now, so exactly when is a crapshoot. Cassie says it's up to nature at this point. Any sign of Eden?"

"Not yet," Hannah said. "Hear anything interesting?"

Angel smirked. "Oh yeah. She lied through her teeth. Ghua

knows it, but he's not pushing her because she played her twelve-year-old card again. He didn't leave that store empty-handed, though. He brought a whole crate of stuff to my house. It's epic. You can come over after this and pick some stuff out."

Hannah grinned and glanced at her fey. His ears darkened, and he frowned at her, looking completely thunderous.

"He thinks Hannah's trying to manipulate him," Angel said, noting my attention. "Tease him with sex to get her way. He still doesn't believe most of her sass is a show now so that she can get her kink scratched on the regular."

Hannah flashed her smile at Angel. "You can't fool me. Soon, that baby belly will be out of the way, and everyone's going to be hearing about your kink."

"Why do you think the toys are at my house?"

Brenna was quietly shaking her head at the pair's banter.

"It's so different here," I said. "In Tenacity, everyone is so focused on supplies and survival. Here it's just sex."

"Pfft. Not true. The trinity of vices—drugs, sex, and alcohol—are everywhere. You just weren't paying attention."

"Isn't it drugs, sex, and gambling?" Brenna asked. "You know, since alcohol falls under the addictive substance category."

Angel just shrugged a shoulder. "Sure, we'll go with that. My point is there's not much else to do. Since Hannah and I aren't drinking, we're down to two vices to entertain ourselves."

"There she is," Hannah said, pointing down the street. "He's carrying her. Full, fey protection mode then." She laughed.

Eden scowled at her the whole way and maintained that

scowl even after Ghua deposited her next to our small circle, kissed her on the cheek, and told her he loved her.

"I love you too, but I'm still twelve."

He sighed, glanced at Hannah, then joined the growing number of fey watching us from the sidelines.

"Can someone explain this 'twelve' thing to me before we get started?" I asked.

"Single females over the age of eighteen are fair game," Brenna said. "Under eighteen are considered children, and fey don't mess with kids. At all."

Hannah crossed her arms and arched a brow at Eden. "Now, spill. I want the details before you channel your rage and hand me my ass today."

"I explained the use of every dildo in the store. There were so many of them that my throat got sore, and I had to stop talking when we got to the other stuff. Ghua packed everything up and brought it back. Fortunately, my voice had enough of a recovery so I could talk to Mya." Eden looked at Angel. "Since you're so open about stuff, Mya designated you as the official gatekeeper. She's going to stop by later to go over the rules, but basically, what you have at your house is not meant for the fey. However, if any of the ladies are interested in anything, she won't stand in the way."

"I feel like I'm some kind of sex toy dealer now," Angel said, rubbing her hands gleefully.

"Because you are," Brenna said flatly. "Expect a visit from my mom soon. Have fun with that. And make sure she's shopping for herself."

Hannah grinned. "Shopping is going to be fun."

"Can we get on with the training already?" Eden begged.

"Sure," Hannah said brightly. "Who do you want to face

first, new girl? Me or the twelve-year-old with the chip on her shoulder?"

Three hours later, I lay on my back, staring at the bright blue sky clouded by my rapid exhales. Hannah's halo of blonde curls and smiling face obliterated my view between one dazed blink and the next.

"Don't worry, Shelby. It takes time."

"That's what I'm afraid of. Everything hurts."

She laughingly took my hand and tugged me to my feet.

"It won't always make you this sore. Stretch when you get home and take a nice hot bath. You'll feel better tomorrow."

I limped my way over to Turik and leaned into his embrace. Thankfully, he got the message, and I didn't have to walk home. Vorx showered with me again and massaged every inch of tired, sore muscle I possessed. Then, they both pampered me further, as promised, and made me brownies while I sat at the island with my head in my hands.

"How can I be so tired?" I complained. "It's barely noon."

"Eat your sandwich," Vorx said. "It will help. Food is fuel."

"I'd rather take a nap."

Thoughts of a daytime snuggle-athon were interrupted by a knock on the door.

"I hope it's not Drav again," I said, suddenly more awake.

Vorx went to answer it while Turik stayed with me, pressing a quick kiss to my temple.

"Hi, is Shelby here?" Emily asked.

Her gaze found mine when Vorx stepped aside.

"Great news," she said with a smile. "You've been officially pardoned. Ready to learn how to sew?"

"I'm not even sure I can lift my arms."

Emily took my jacket from the entry and came toward me.

"Hannah said she tried to take it easy on you but that you weren't getting your arms up fast enough. I thought I'd introduce you to something a little more peaceful. Trust me when I say you'll want to keep moving around for a bit, or you'll get stiff."

She had me in my jacket and shoes and out the door before I knew what was happening.

CHAPTER TWENTY-SEVEN

Vorx and Turik trailed behind us, going along with the flow.

"The group was big enough that we split into two," Emily explained. "Julie is hosting one group at her house, and I'm hosting the other. Fifteen in each. Can you believe that?"

"No?" I still wasn't sure what was going on.

"It's insane how quickly willingness is changing now. June said it's still chaotic over there with the continuation of the housing reshuffle, but she spoke with each volunteer coming here and explained your presence. No one had any problems. A lot of support, actually. Apparently, your ex didn't have too many fans."

"Can't imagine why," I said dryly.

Emily nodded. "Yeah, I'm glad there weren't more people following his way of thinking. June said that there are a lot of fey coming and going now. They're still doing the soup kitchen method of feeding everyone while they organize the schedule for supply runs. But, when June heard we were looking for people with some trade skills, she put a sign-up list at the beginning of the soup kitchen line yesterday. People got an extra biscuit if they could come up with five things they could do well. Everyone got an extra biscuit. But it turns out that Sam, June's new housemate, knows how to knit. She's going to be teaching us today."

My head was spinning with that outpouring of information.

"I thought June was living with a fey," I said, still trying to catch up.

"Oh, she is. Sam asked if she could live with them to see what living with a fey would be like. It's part of the whole intermingling thing. If it's anything like my experience, she's going to be wearing headphones an awful lot." She gave me a sheepish look. "It's not something I'll ask you to do. Dealing with two fey at once would scare away too many women."

"What's Julie's group learning?" I asked, changing the subject.

"It's a cooking class. Just the basics to see if anyone has talent." She hesitated a moment, her steps slowing. "Would you rather go to that class?"

"No, knitting is fine. I was just curious. Asking Julie to lead cooking makes sense. She's an amazing cook," I said, thinking of her beef roast dinner.

"She is," Emily agreed. "There will probably be some left if you want to stop in for a bite. Her door is always open to everyone."

Not having to cook sounded divine since I wasn't sure how I was going to stay awake for a knitting lesson, never mind dinner. But I knew Vorx and Turik wouldn't let me starve.

I glanced over my shoulder at them. Turik flashed his teeth back at me. Vorx's gaze swept me head to toe like he was seeing every sign of just how tired I was, from the drag in my step to the droop of my shoulders. I gave him a reassuring smile and focused on Emily's conversation. Thankfully, we arrived at her house before I had to beg one of my guys for a ride.

"Are you two staying for the lessons, or are you going to go enjoy a bit of freedom around town?" she asked as we moved up the front walk.

"We will stay," Turik said.

"You sure?" she asked. "Even Merdon hightailed it out of here when he heard how many women would be present."

"Women?" Vorx asked.

Feeling a whole heap of uncertainty, I glanced back at him.

"Maybe you want to stay and meet a few?" I asked as Emily opened the door.

The heat from inside gusted out, along with the murmur of conversation coming from over a dozen people crowded into her living room.

"I already met the woman I want," Vorx said, coming toward me. "She is beautiful and courageous and has many things she doesn't wish to talk about."

Oh, that smirk again. It did wicked things to my insides and planted thoughts in my head that didn't belong there.

He palmed the back of my neck, and I tipped my head back, ready to give him my lips.

"I will kiss her when I see her at home tonight," he said softly. "When she begs for it."

Emily laughed lightly. "You can blame the begging thing on Hannah. When Merdon figured out how to drive her wild, he told everyone."

Vorx kissed the tip of my nose and stepped back so Turik could swoop in and give me a light kiss on the lips. Then they were gone.

"Come on. I'll introduce you."

I knew more than half of the women by name already and had seen the rest around Tenacity at some point. They smiled and said polite things while their eyes reflected a burning curiosity. I couldn't be sure if it was due to the dual goodbyes they witnessed at the door or because I was now living with my ex's hated enemies. Either way, I didn't much care and focused on Sam's knitting lessons.

Time passed with quiet conversation, a few groans of frustration, and the general clack of knitting needles. The skill escaped me. Maybe I was too tired or simply didn't enjoy it enough to try harder. Either way, the pattern was loose in some spots, tight in others, and I tended to mess up the counts.

Two hours later, we called it quits. I wasn't sad to unravel my attempt so someone else could reuse the yarn. Two ladies in the group went home with their knitting needles, and one had a semblance of a mitten going.

Outside, the fey were waiting like timeshare salesmen to talk the women into a ride home. Emily and I watched the women get whisked away one by one with far less reluctance than I would have expected. A few of the ones I knew waved goodbye.

Hannah went outside, looked both ways, then took off at a run.

Emily closed the door with a laugh, and I returned to the couch to wait for my guys to show up.

"So, what do you think? Are you going to try again tomorrow?" she asked.

"Knitting? Probably not. I don't think I have the patience for it. I'd rather find something I can do outside. Like gardening.

Great for summer, but not so great for this time of year. Too bad we don't have a greenhouse or something."

"Let your guys know you want one, and they'll find you something. Or build it." Her gaze lit with excitement. "It wouldn't be a bad thing to get started. Julie's been collecting canning supplies, but I know people are hungry for fresh greens again. Mary and I were experimenting with growing sprouts. We even did some lettuce. Nothing large scale, but if you could manage it, there sure would be a lot of people willing to trade."

"I'll let them know," I promised. "So, where did Hannah run off to?"

"Angel's, if I were to guess. She's toying with Merdon, which is her new favorite pastime. That man is crazy in love with her but doesn't put up with any of her crap, which is really good for her. However, that means the two of them sometimes butt heads. Right now, she's trying to mess with his favorite way of snapping her out of her funks."

"I don't understand."

"Merdon trains Hannah like you trained this morning. Only it's a lot harder because he's fey and fast and strong." She waved her hand. "You get what I mean. Anyway, he spanks her when she doesn't defend herself well enough. It's an incentive to try harder.

"She's going to Angel's to get a butt plug. I'm not sure if she'll actually use it or if she just wants it in the house so Merdon will wonder if it's in and be in a constant state of arousal. Like he's not already." Emily shook her head. "Seriously, they're at it all the time. Eight rounds in one day last week. Her all-time high."

I hesitated only a minute before sharing.

"Turik and Vorx talk a lot about limits and that Eden has to ice afterward."

Emily grinned. "Ghua is more sex-obsessed than the average fey, I think. I heard he finagled twelve rounds out of her in one day, and four were oral."

I cringed.

"Yeah, that was my thought, too. But Hannah swears the fey are magic and the things they can make a girl feel are worth it. And they're getting smarter about breaks for restorative baths and icing."

"And I have two of them?" I said, a little worried for myself.

"Never forget the power of 'No,'" Emily said with a pat to my hand.

Hannah breezed in several minutes later.

"Look who I found at Angel's," she said, holding the door for Vorx and Turik. "And guess what they were looking at." She held up a pink and black box with a cellophane window that left no doubt what held their interest. "Don't worry. Angel didn't let them take one. You're safe."

Turik looked like a kid busted stealing cookies. Vorx's expression was carefully blank as he watched for my reaction.

"Still not a topic open for discussion," I said calmly. "Normal first."

Both fey grunted.

"Yeah, smart move," Hannah said. "I think it's better to let Eden be the first female to give in to it. That girl's vagina is going to break soon if Ghua can't find another hole to fill."

"Hannah, please," Emily said. "Use your eyes. Shelby's uncomfortable with this topic."

Hannah's expression immediately shifted to remorse.

"Hey, I'm sorry."

"It's okay. I kind of like how open everyone is about things going on behind closed doors. It feels safer in a way."

Hannah moved to sit beside me. "I heard about your bruises and can imagine what happened behind your closed doors," she said with a brutal honesty that painfully laid me bare.

"I tried killing myself not too long ago," she continued. "Actually, I was killing myself slowly long before that. Brenna gave me some advice that I didn't believe. She told me to talk about it. She said the more it hurt, the more I didn't want to talk about it, the more I needed to get it out. She was right. So, I might be a little too open now in my attempts to purge everything and fix the mess that it still feels like I have going on up here." She tapped her temple. "If you ever need a non-judgmental ear, I'll listen. So will Emily, Brenna, her mom... Hell, there isn't a woman in Tolerance who wouldn't wrap you in a hug and listen to your story." She patted my knee. "Whenever you're ready."

"Thanks."

"Meanwhile, I highly recommend sex therapy and feight club. If I can't exercise it out of you there, they'll be able to wear you out in the bedroom."

"Hannah, you were doing so well," Emily said with an amused shake of her head.

The door opened suddenly, and Merdon strode in, looking as angry as ever.

Hannah popped up from her spot on the couch and lifted the box in her palm. Her smile never wavered from her face as he stalked toward her.

"I am not trying to manipulate you. I love you, and I want to experience something new and maybe very enjoyable with you. It might hurt, though. So, you'll need to be careful with me the first time. Want to go upstairs and try this out?"

"Yeah, I don't think headphones are going to be enough for this one. I'm heading to Mary and James's."

"James and Mary aren't taking visitors for a while," Turik said. "Mary heard our questions and said Randy Stallion was going to be visiting, and she wouldn't be up for company after the ride."

"What were you asking about?" Emily asked.

Turik and Vorx shared a look then stared at me.

Understanding dawned.

"Anal sex," I said.

"Oh, God. I think I just threw up in my mouth," Hannah said with a horrified look on her face. "This is going to have to wait." She tossed the box over her shoulder and went to the kitchen. "Where's the therapy chocolate?"

Emily's face was stunned, and she didn't answer.

Merdon walked over to Hannah and found the chocolate she was frantically searching for.

"Who is Randy Stallion, and why is his visit upsetting Hannah?" Turik said, coming to stand beside me.

CHAPTER TWENTY-EIGHT

HANNAH PLUGGED HER EARS AND STARTED SINGING.

"That's not something I'm prepared to explain," I said calmly. "I think it's time for us to go home."

Emily managed a weak goodbye as we left. Hannah was too busy asking the ceiling, "Why?" to notice.

"The topic I don't really want to discuss is something that I'd say at least half of all women don't want to consider. Ever. Which means that it's a sensitive topic that needs to be approached with care. Definitely not something to discuss in mixed company. Do you understand? Be careful who you talk to and who can hear, or you might upset someone."

Both fey grunted but still looked confused.

"Did James and Mary at least answer your questions?"

"Yes. James explained how it's done and what we would need. He also said it might not work because of our size," Vorx said.

"He didn't think it would kill you," Turik said quickly. "And he had many suggestions for how to prepare you before we tried. Which is why we went to Angel's. We wanted to see—"

"Still not ready to talk about this, guys."

I got another unison grunt in response.

Back home, I closed myself in the bathroom to take the shower I'd wanted after Hannah's grueling workout. The door opened when I was rinsing the conditioner from my hair, but no one was there when I shut off the water and looked out. However, a whole candy bar waited for me on top of a pair of sweatpants and a sweatshirt.

"Is this therapy chocolate?" I called.

"Yes," Turik said from the other side of the door.

I grinned a little, understanding that they were trying to make me comfortable again.

"Any chance you'd be willing to come in here and help me dry off?"

The door immediately opened, and Turik strode in. He accepted the towel I offered and took over drying me. I grinned at him the entire time. It didn't take him long to smile back.

"You missed a spot here." I pointed to the underside of my breast.

He patted it again, and I shook my head.

"Still feels damp. Maybe you should check with your lips."

He lifted me and kissed me where I'd indicated, then licked and nipped the spot. I sighed contentedly and closed my eyes.

"Yeah, just like that."

I felt him turn and start walking while he continued his teasing attention on my breast. When he eased me back onto a mattress, I stretched my arms over my head and arched into his mouth.

"Make me scream in a good way," I said softly.

He growled in response, not veering from his task, as he nudged my legs apart. His mouth teased one breast while he used his hand to toy with the other. My nipples hardened, begging for attention.

I heard a creak nearby. Opening my eyes, I turned my head to find Vorx sitting in a chair.

"You are so pretty, Shelby," he said, his gaze skimming over me. "The nipple Turik wants to devour is pink in agreement. Do you want his mouth there yet?"

I did, and I didn't. I loved the teasing and the waiting because I knew how much better it would feel in the end. Vorx saw my hesitation and chuckled.

"Not yet, then," he said as I closed my eyes and let myself drift in the feeling of Turik's mouth on me.

The flickering need climbed higher with each lick and nip. Heat flushed my skin, and my breathing grew shallower. When his hand left my breast and skimmed my inner thigh, I parted my legs for him, eager for his touch there as well. At that moment, I could understand why Eden gave in so many times. I was addicted to Turik's touch—both of their touches, really—and couldn't imagine ever walking away from this.

His fingers skimmed over my folds at first then teased my opening. I spread wider in response, knocking a knee into his chest. His hand left me as he shifted his position to give me more room, but not his mouth. That stayed where it was and brushed over a nipple. My lips parted in anticipation of his tongue and teeth, but neither came. Instead, he licked and nipped the underside of the other breast.

A disgruntled sound escaped me, and he chuckled.

"Patience," he whispered before his fingers returned to my folds.

He toyed with me, edging ever closer to my clit, only to skate away. The need for him to do something more grew stronger. My hands drifted down to his head, and I threaded my fingers in his hair.

"Yes," he purred. "Show me what you want."

I guided his head to my first breast.

"Here?" he asked, his warm breath washing over the peak.

"Yes."

He moved just to the left to lift and nipped at the same time his finger dipped to my entrance, diverting any disappointment I felt over his miss. I raised my hips, more than ready to welcome his touch, but he moved away from that too.

Another frustrated sound escaped me.

"Tell me what you want, Shelby. Do you want my kisses here and here"—he kissed my breast and tapped my clit—"to make you scream, or do you want more?" His tongue flicked my nipple. Then he kissed a slow path down my stomach. "Do you want to feel me move inside of you?"

"Yes. All of it," I said, breathing harder as his warm exhale washed over my core. I would have given anything, made any promise, just to feel him there. Turik was too sweet to take advantage of me like that, though, no matter how much I wanted him to.

Instead, he lowered his head and gave me a slow lick from core to clit that made me squirm and arch into the sensations. The pleasure climbed higher inside of me, and just when I thought I would topple over the edge, his mouth left me.

I opened my eyes and saw him kneeling between my legs. Naked and large, his muscles flexed as he prowled up my body and locked his mouth over one tight nipple. After waiting so long, the suction I'd craved brought both pleasure and an ache that made me feel both needful and woefully bereft.

My core clenched around nothing when his teeth scraped me, and I mewled.

"Turik. Please."

"Shh. Soon."

He took my other breast into his mouth, sucking just a little harder. The sound that tore from my throat was just a little louder when he released it and gave the taut point a gentle bite. He licked the flat of his tongue over it then kissed his way up my neck.

"Tell me what you want," he said.

Since he didn't seem inclined to listen, I didn't speak. I simply reached between us and clasped his hot length, stroking it while imagining how it would feel when he was finally inside of me. He wasn't only long; he was thick, and I would feel every inch of him long after he was done and gone.

"You, Turik. I want you." I reached for that spot he liked and smiled at his hissed exhale. His hands clasped my thighs, pressing them wide, and I watched him position himself at my entrance.

He wasn't moving fast enough for my liking, and I arched up.

"Slow, Shelby."

His head stretched me, and he grunted as he watched it disappear.

"So hot and tight." He pressed forward, giving me another inch. "And wet."

Then he closed his eyes. I did the same, focusing on each gloriously veined inch he worked into me. He filled me completely then demanded more, stretching me to the point of discomfort. Somehow, he knew and retreated, only to ease forward again. And again. And again, until my body gave him what he wanted.

Everything.

He growled, and I moaned when he finally seated himself fully. I'd never felt anything like it before. So full. So perfect. I could understand why the other women kept saying yes.

Then he started thrusting. Nerve endings I didn't know I had zinged with pleasure, drawing that tenuous string of pleasure tighter and tighter until it snapped. I convulsed, opening my mouth in a silent scream as the first wave of my orgasm washed over me. There was no sound. Only joy.

The hot jolt of his release coated my insides, adding to the carnality, and I bucked under him, determined to ring out every ounce of pleasure he could give me.

I wasn't sure how long it lasted, but eventually, we both calmed and lay together breathless and sweaty.

"You're too heavy to lie on her like that. Get off."

Turik kissed me soundly before rolling next to me. Vorx scooped me up from the bed. I didn't open my eyes to look at him. I couldn't.

He walked with me, shifted my weight to one arm, and I heard the shower start. A moment later, the warm spray was hitting my side and lap. His hand slipped between my legs and gently washed me. However, every light brush of his fingers against my sex sent an overly intense aftershock of pleasure through me.

"Stop," I managed, swatting his hand away.

"Was he too rough with you?" he asked with concern.

I opened my eyes to look at him.

"No, he was just right. But I'd like a kiss from you now so I know you're okay with what happened."

Vorx leaned in and kissed me tenderly, yet with so much emotion that I never wanted to leave his arms.

"I am more than okay with what happened, Shelby," he said when he pulled away. "You were beautiful to watch." He kissed my brow. "I hope you never want to leave because I don't think I will ever be able to let you go."

"Sweet man," I said softly.

He kissed me again on the lips, making my heart ache, then eased me to my feet so I could finish washing alone. I wasn't even a little sore. Everything felt too good for that yet.

Relaxed and smiling to myself as I relived how amazing that had been, I left the shower. My clothes were already in the bathroom, along with Turik, who held a towel.

He dried me carefully between peppering my face with random kisses, and when he reached my breasts, he playfully used his mouth to verify he'd dried them correctly. This time, he didn't teasingly avoid the nipples but carefully drew them into his mouth, soothing them with his tongue. My core clenched but with less intensity. After he finished leisurely inspecting both of them, he pulled me into his arms.

"I need to hear you say it again. Was I too rough? Does anything hurt?"

"I've never felt so good in my life, Turik. I swear."

He planted a kiss on the tip of my nose.

"Vorx will try to do better."

"I will do better," Vorx called from the other room.

"But not today," Turik called back.

The bathroom door opened.

"Not today," Vorx agreed. "Go shower. I will care for Shelby."

Turik gave me another face.

"I want to keep touching you. You better go, or I will kiss you until you beg me to make you scream again." He shrugged. "I can't decide which hungers for you more. My cock or tongue?"

Vorx unwedged me from Turik's hold.

"Both will need to wait. Shelby needs rest first."

"I don't know," I said. "Shelby's tits are tingling, and she's thinking another round wouldn't be the worst idea. She also doesn't like when you talk about her like she's not here."

Turik laughed, a deep, delighted sound.

Vorx picked me up and strode out of the bathroom.

"Does this mean it's your turn next?" I asked, reaching up to run a finger along his ear.

His gaze pinned me.

"Soon."

CHAPTER TWENTY-NINE

I LAY ON THE COUCH, CONTENT FOR THE FIRST TIME IN A VERY LONG time. Worries about food, safety, the future couldn't touch me, not with my fey ensuring I had everything I'd ever wanted. Turik rubbed my feet, occasionally running a finger along my arch just to see me twitch and giggle, and Vorx brushed my hair in long, languid strokes.

There wasn't another place on the planet where I would rather be. A movie played on the TV, but I wasn't watching it. I was basking in fey affection. Life was, for the first time in my life, perfect.

I sighed gustily and tipped my head back to look at Vorx.

"I can hear your stomach growling. How long are you willingly going to starve just so you don't disturb me?"

"Forever."

I shook my head at him.

"If you starve, you can't take care of me. Take care of yourself too. Okay?"

Neither tried to stop me from sitting up. I stretched and stood.

"What are you hungry for tonight?" I asked, looking at Vorx.

"You."

"You're the one who keeps saying soon. I'm here whenever you want me." I shot him a sassy look and exaggerated my walk all the way to the kitchen. A growl sounded behind me, and two steely arms wrapped around my waist. He spun us around and nibbled on my neck as I laughed.

When he finally stopped, I was breathless, dizzy, and clinging to him.

"Soon," he whispered in my ear. Then he caught it between his teeth in a gentle bite before releasing me and grabbing the cookbook.

Breathlessly, I watched him page through the recipes, looking at the images. He and Turik might have given me a home, but they'd also made one for themselves in my very soul. They owned me in ways that Nat had wanted to but never could. I craved their touch, their attention, their love. They consumed my thoughts and gave me a reason to exist. Their love for me was enough to keep me here forever, and I desperately wanted to show them that.

We worked together to prepare the meal again. My praise for a job well done—no matter how small—was a hand rubbed over the front of the pants and a kiss to the cheek.

Turik had trouble sitting when it was finally time to eat. Vorx wasn't much better off, but his hot gaze and tight smirk promised retribution. I welcomed it with open arms because I knew what I'd find in his. Only pleasure. Never pain.

So, I used my foot to torment him as I ate. Turik chuckled, understanding what I was doing based on Vorx's steady stare and hissed out breaths.

Halfway through my meal, I pushed my chair away from the table.

"Excuse me for a minute. I'll be right back." I set my hand on Vorx's shoulder as I passed. "Eat while you can."

Turik chuckled again, and as I walked away, I heard him say, "I told you our Shelby had fire buried inside of her."

In my room, I hurriedly ditched the sweatshirt and sweatpants and changed into Vorx's favorite outfit—the thong and see-through shirt.

"Dinner was delicious, but I think I'd like to save the rest of mine for later," I said when I returned.

Both men stopped eating and watched me cross the room. I looked pointedly at Vorx.

"You didn't eat enough. Taking care of each other goes both ways. I'm going to think you don't have the strength to carry me if you don't eat."

He absently brought his fork to his mouth and ate the bite of meat on it. I doubted he tasted anything, though. His eyes tracked me as I walked to the fridge with my plate.

"Now, where did I see that cling wrap?" I asked, bending at the waist to look in a cabinet that I knew did not have any form of food wrap.

A chair scraped the floor behind me, and I grinned at the same time hands gripped my hips.

"Wait," I said firmly.

His hands stayed on my hips, but he didn't do anything more. I glanced over my shoulder at him then leaned farther to the side to see his almost untouched plate. Turik winked at me.

"You didn't eat," I said, looking at Vorx.

"I'm not hungry."

"Well, that's too bad. I guess Turik can have your serving of pussy for dessert."

Turik roared with laughter.

Vorx's response was to toss me over his shoulder and stride to my bedroom.

"Wait," I said, stopping him in the hallway. "I want to walk from here. Please."

He growled a frustrated sound but immediately released me.

"Thank you," I said primly.

I swayed my hips as I walked to the bed, then climbed onto the mattress on my hands and knees. Staying near the edge, I glanced over my shoulder at Vorx, who stood two steps behind me, staring at my ass.

The chair next to the bed creaked, but I didn't look away from Vorx.

"Is it soon yet?" I asked.

In response, he pulled his shirt off in one smooth motion and tossed it aside. Then, he leaned over me, blanketing my back with his chiseled bare chest. His teeth scraped my neck, and he whispered close to my ear.

"Will you trust me?"

"Always," I said, already breathless.

He kissed his way down my back, skipping the use of his tongue and teeth until he reached my ass. His hands kneaded my curves then jerked my legs out from under me.

"Gently, Vorx. Her bruises are still fading," Turik warned even as Vorx gave another tug, aligning my hips with the edge of the bed.

My already racing pulse kicked it up another notch.

"Maybe not all the way gentle," I said with a glance at each of them.

Vorx said something in another language, and Turik grunted. Then Vorx spread my legs wide and knelt behind me.

I held my breath, waiting for what he'd do, and gripped the sheets. He kissed the underside of my right cheek, then licked and nipped it. I loved his fascination with my backside and the hinted edge of danger in it.

His exhale washed over my skin near where he'd nipped, and my core clenched hard in anticipation of the next scrape of his teeth. He surprised me by feathering his fingers over the narrow strip of cloth covering my folds but didn't attempt to tug it aside. He was simply letting me know he was there and thinking about what he wanted to do, which got me thinking about what I wanted him to do, too. The answer involved a lot more than his attentive mouth and fingers. Though, I adored those too.

He resumed his kiss, lick, and bite assault until he'd covered the entire surface of my right cheek, and I squirmed and sought more than that light touch between my legs. I thought for sure he'd shift his focus to the other side and tease me further.

Instead, he finally slid his fingers under the material. He didn't explore my folds like I desperately wanted, though. He hooked a finger around the material, brushing his knuckle over my clit in the process. I bucked against him, and he kissed my other cheek.

"Shh," he soothed. "Soon."

He slowly dragged his knuckle down my clit to my core, skimming over that small space of transition where the material stopped and the string began, then over the place no man belonged.

A shiver ran through me, and I clenched back there at the contact, surprised at the explosion of desire the contact caused.

He continued tracing his way until he reached the waistband then gently tugged them down my legs, giving me a minute to close my legs and compose myself. I didn't need time, though. I knew Vorx wasn't pushing for more. He was asking for me to trust him and his respect for me. For now, my answer was no—maybe it would always be—and he was okay with that. But as Turik had pointed out, Vorx liked to tease regardless.

So, I returned my legs to their spread position, no string hiding me from his view.

"Thank you," he whispered before he began worshiping the left side of the physical attribute he adored.

Panting, I focused on Turik, who was scrutinizing my expression for any hint of discomfort. I gave him a small smile and hummed my pleasure.

"Thank you," Turik echoed. "For trusting us to care for you."

I opened my mouth to answer, but Vorx slipped a hand under my hips and started circling my clit. All thought died, and I began to short-circuit when his tongue thrust into me.

"Ungh."

"She likes that very much," Turik murmured.

Vorx fed his tongue deeper then withdrew. A moment later, something much larger prodded my entrance. He groaned and pushed forward slowly, not having the patience Turik had. Vorx didn't pause when my body resisted the oversized intrusion. He simply withdrew and tried again, working his way in until his hips snapped forward, and he thrust home.

"More," I panted. I didn't want slow and tender from Vorx. I wanted hard and fast. I wanted to feel him there when I woke up the next day. He read my need and started a steady, pounding rhythm. I panted and arched, focused on that slow tightening inside of me, fed by each slick slide of his hard length and stroke of his finger.

He lifted me suddenly and turned to sit on the bed. My knees rested on the mattress, giving me some control. I picked up the pace and drove down harder. His fingers circled my clit faster, and his other hand found my breast. Plaintive, desperate sounds escaped from my lips, but I didn't let up. I was driven and in need.

A moment later, my orgasm ripped through me.

Vorx flipped me over again and pounded into me. The slap of his thighs against my ass filled the room, along with Turik's voice. I was too high on pleasure to care about anything more than the feel of Vorx swelling inside of me until he jerked to a stop and hissed out an angry sound with the first explosion of his release.

Lips touched my eyelids, and with a dazed smile, I briefly wondered when I'd closed them.

"Shelby? Are you okay?" Turik asked.

"So good," I murmured, my pulse still pounding loudly in my ears.

Vorx was still hard inside of me, but he'd stopped twitching.

"Is there more?" I asked.

"Do you want more?"

"Yes, please."

I yawned.

"Can you open your eyes?"

"No. I can have sex with my eyes closed, though. I'm that good."

Vorx leaned over me and kissed my neck.

"So good," he whispered. "But we'll need to wait for tomorrow for more."

I made a sad face, and Turik started peppering my brow and cheeks with kisses.

"Patience, Shelby," Vorx said. "Eden said that Ghua played with his favorite toy so much he almost broke it."

"His favorite toy is her pussy," Turik clarified. "We don't want to break yours."

I opened my eyes and grinned at him.

"Thank you for your consideration."

He grunted and kissed my nose.

"Tomorrow," he promised.

The next morning, Turik kept his word. While lying in a puddle of happy, I asked if they were keeping track of who went last and how taking turns would work with their three orgasms a day rule. They clarified that number was only my training wheels rule. They fully hoped to increase my daily orgasms based on what I could handle.

Since my guys were so carefully gentle, I knew I would be taking on Eden's eight-a-day max rule. Vorx and Turik paid attention to my whole body so specific parts wouldn't get too overstimulated and sore. And after swatting Vorx's hand away the day before, they fully trusted me to say when enough was enough.

But I was discovering I had a greedy side and doubted I would ever have enough of them.

CHAPTER THIRTY

I WALKED TO THE TRAINING GROUNDS WITH A SPRING IN MY STEP and my hand in Vorx's, once again teasing him with long looks and accidental brushes.

"Morning," Angel called when she spotted me. "Late start?"

I grinned. "Early start actually, just an unplanned distraction."

Turning to Vorx, I tipped my head up for his hungry kiss. Turik chuckled at my dazed expression when Vorx released me and kissed my temple before they both moved off to the side.

"Come on, lover girl," Angel said, hooking her arm through mine. "Eden's still fighting mean, and Hannah needs a friend."

"I am not fighting mean," Eden said. "I'm fighting to win, and payback is going to be a bitch."

Hannah snorted and motioned for me to stretch with her.

A short while later, I learned that Hannah's idea of friendship was mocking my attempts to block her about two seconds prior to flipping me onto my back.

Again and again.

"I need a time out and a change in fighting technique," I panted. "Distance is more my thing."

Brenna laughingly handed me Angel's bow.

"Step right up."

Brenna was just as torturous, though. My arm felt like it wanted to fall off by the time she finally told me to take a break. I sat on the stump next to Angel.

"Can't I just be a professional eater like you?" I asked.

Grinning, she withdrew yet another snack cake from one of her pockets and handed it to me.

"Your kid is going to come out with vanilla filling if you don't lay off of these," I said, opening my own.

"See, Shax! Even the new girl knows I'm eating too many of these things. Fruit-based snacks next time. I mean it."

"It had a strawberry on the box."

She sighed and looked at me. "He is so incredibly sweet."

I grinned and bit into my snack cake. Even pregnant and sore, Angel never got short with Shax. It was clear that they loved each other to pieces.

A call went out somewhere else in the neighborhood. While it sounded urgent, the fey around us grunted and grinned.

"What was that?" I asked when Hannah stopped what she was doing and picked up her bow.

"Crap. They're early. Be at Emily's in an hour," she said, pointing at me. "You can pretend to care about knitting and keep me company."

Angel chuckled and waited until Merdon was jogging after Hannah before explaining.

"The group from Tenacity is coming," Angel said, standing with a wince. "They're driving here today. Two trucks. Some of the people—women mostly—are staying here for the training that Emily coordinated. Half the fey are either running to get in line to carry a female or gathering around Emily's and Julie's to start the lines to carry them home."

"You said some of the people are staying here. What about the rest?"

"Ryan asked for more volunteers to help set up the new place. Once the drivers drop off their passengers, the remaining people are loading up some of the extra supplies we have here and heading out again. Stay away from the storage shed for a few hours. It's going to be chaos."

"It sounds like I won't have any free time until dinner, anyway. But thanks for the warning. See you tomorrow."

I waved goodbye to Brenna and let Turik carry me home. He asked twice what hurt and how tired I was, but I assured him I wasn't overly sore or tired, even though I did have a few aches.

As soon as we were in the house, I used my own two feet to walk to the bedroom, shedding my clothing along the way. A glance over my shoulder showed Vorx only a step behind, and I had his full attention.

A short time later, I lay back on top of Vorx. His hard length continued to twitch inside of me as his chest rose and fell with his harsh breathing. My chest did the same.

Legs spread over Vorx's, I lifted my head and looked at Turik, who watched me closely.

"Nothing hurts, and that wasn't too rough," I said before he could ask.

It'd been deliciously hard and fast. Just what I'd needed.

"Is this like swimming? Do I need to wait an hour before asking to dive in again after my first helping?"

"For now," Turik said, his hungry gaze taking me in. Based

on the way he palmed his hard length, he didn't seem to mind the view of Vorx still inside of me. Not at all.

I eased off of Vorx, kissed him deeply, and moved to the bathroom. Turik was right behind me and washed my hair while I ran my hands over his water-slicked chest.

When he finished, I convinced him with my mouth that I didn't need an hour restriction. Vorx came in when I was pinned against the wall screaming my third orgasm for the day, shook his head at Turik, and called him weak.

"I would like to see you resist her mouth on your cock," Turik said without a hint of offense.

"Challenge accepted," Vorx said with a grin through the shower door. "Now, let our Shelby down so she can finish washing."

My legs were weak, and it took a few minutes to clean myself. However, Vorx was still waiting to dry me when I finished. He gazed into my eyes for a long moment, looking like he wanted to say something.

"What is it?" I asked.

He exhaled a content sound and kissed me on the nose.

"Nothing. Get dressed, or you will be late."

Turik had lunch waiting for me on the counter. A sandwich again.

It didn't puzzle me how something so simple could be that amazingly delicious. Going without and having too many near-death experiences made every positive aspect of life taste that much better.

"What are you two going to do while I'm pretending to knit?" I asked between bites.

They shared one of their looks again.

"Please don't tell me you're going to go back to James and Mary's. Or Angel's."

"No. We wanted to look for more supplies since most of them are going to the new place. Would you feel safe if we left? There will be twenty fey protecting Emily and Hannah's house."

"I will feel completely safe in a house full of people surrounded by fey. Go do your part."

"I ASKED Merdon if I could start carrying around a set of knitting needles," Hannah said conversationally. "They'd make handy stab weapons. He told me they would get too slippery, though, so he's going to come up with something like them but with handles."

She grinned at my "ew" face.

"You need a healthy hobby," I said. "Something that doesn't revolve around fighting and killing."

"I already have one. It's called sex."

Emily shot Hannah a scolding look and glanced at the clock.

"All right," Emily called over the group's quiet conversation. "Our time's up for today. Julie's group was baking the biscuits for tonight's community stew pot, so we don't want to hold them up."

We started unraveling what we'd done and surrendered our yarn.

This time, my fey were with the group waiting outside when Emily opened the door.

"See you in the morning," Hannah called.

I waved goodbye and went straight to Turik for a

welcoming hug. How could a few hours apart feel like a lifetime? He wrapped his arms around me and placed a kiss on the top of my head. Closing my eyes, I soaked up his warmth and love before pulling back to smile up at him and Vorx, who stood beside him.

"I missed you guys."

"Are you tired?" Turik asked.

"Nope. A little restless from sitting so long without you guys." I held his hand. "How did it go looking for supplies? Find anything good?"

He glanced at Vorx, who slowly smirked at me. A bolt of need flared in my middle at the heat in his gaze.

"Does that mean you're not going to tell me?" I asked.

"We will show you when we get home," Turik said.

I walked with them to the house, anticipation filling me.

The moment I opened the door, the scent of roasted meat and vegetables hit me, and my stomach growled.

"Did you guys cook without me?" I asked while Vorx helped me out of my jacket.

"No," Turik said. "We stopped at Julie's for dinner when we returned so you could eat right away. We have a lot to do tonight."

I looked between the pair, trying to figure out what was up.

"The suspense is killing me. What did you two find?"

Vorx's arms closed around my torso, lifting me so he could kiss the back of my neck and palm a breast while his erection ground against my ass.

Grinning like an idiot, I hooked my arms around his neck and reveled in the feel of his mouth while he held me. Something thumped on the counter, snapping me out of the sexual haze slowly consuming me. I glanced at the box of chocolate cake mix and the gallon container of ice cream Turik had placed on the counter.

"You can have your cake and eat it," Turik said.

"Every day for the rest of your life," Vorx added, nibbling at the back of my neck.

My heart melted at their sweet gesture.

"You left to find cake and ice cream for me?"

"And something for us," Vorx murmured, nipping my skin and arching into me.

"I like where this is going," I said breathlessly.

My gaze locked with Turik, and I extended a hand to him. He closed the distance between us and kissed me hard. I wrapped my legs around his waist, loving both their attention.

Unfortunately, it ended too soon.

"Go upstairs and change," Vorx said, releasing me and giving my backside a motivating swat.

Confused and more than a little curious, I hurried to the bedroom and found one of them had laid out some new clothes for me. The bra, if it could be called that since it was missing the cups, was a series of interwoven straps that would leave most of my breasts exposed. The bottoms were also missing material.

A slow smile curved my lips as I stared at the outfit and understood what their gifts meant. They wanted me to know I could have it all. I could keep the home I'd made with them, the feeling of safety, and have both of them in my life in any way I wanted.

They wouldn't be disappointed if I chose not to wear the outfit. They would continue to love me on my terms. But I didn't want that. I wanted them to love me on their terms, too.

I hurried to dress, and feeling sexy as hell, I sashayed my way to the kitchen.

Both fey watched me hungrily, ignoring the food they'd dished up while waiting for me. Lifting my arms, I executed a slow turn for them so they could see what they'd given me.

"Thank you for the clothes."

"Thank you for wearing them," Turik said, reaching out to run his fingers over my breasts.

"Should we eat first? The food looks too good to waste."

Turik made me laugh by taking his seat and wolfing down several large bites. He nudged Vorx, who was still staring at me.

"Sit. Eat. The faster we finish, the sooner we can start."

Vorx held out his hand to me and guided me to my chair, his intense, hungry gaze sweeping over me from head to toe, missing nothing. Part of me wanted to take back what I'd said about eating first, but my stomach growled, and I knew neither of them would let me postpone eating.

It should have felt weird sitting practically bare-assed on the stool, but it didn't. It felt naughty and sexy with the way both of them watched me.

I took a bite, savoring the gravy-soaked shredded beef's flavor.

"This is so good," I said after I swallowed.

They grunted and methodically attacked their double portions. I had only managed half of mine by the time they finished theirs but didn't hesitate to push back my plate.

"I'll save that for later."

Vorx swept me off the chair and started toward the living room, where someone had had the forethought to draw the shades.

"What are you—"

His lips crashed on mine with an urgency that made me tingle in all the best places. I moaned lightly and kissed him with just as much hunger, showing him how much I'd missed him while he'd been away and how much I adored what they'd done for me.

My backside hit the couch. Then his lips left mine, trailing their way down my chest. There was no licking and nipping— just the wet heat of his mouth on my breast and the flick of his tongue.

I slid my fingers into his hair and arched into him. Everything in me relaxed at the same time like someone flicked a switch.

The magic of a fey tongue, I thought to myself as I floated in a sea of desire.

He left my breast for the other and nudged my knees apart. I lifted my legs to set my heels on the couch and give him all the access he could want but missed. He caught my ankle and helped me lift my foot to the cushion.

Thoughts of how heavy my legs felt drifted away when he lifted his head, looked down at me, and growled.

"Pretty pussy," he said.

But the words sounded off. Slurred.

"Vorx? Is something wrong?" I asked.

My words didn't sound quite right, either.

He shook his head like he was trying to rattle some thoughts loose, then dipped his head to lick me from opening to mound. Pleasure swirled deliciously, and forgetting everything, I closed my eyes, briefly letting my mind swim in the sensation. When I opened them again, the room spun a little like I was drunk, which only made what he was doing more enjoyable.

"Yeah, like that," I said.

I turned my head to look for Turik.

He was frowning and trying to stand up.

"Come here," I murmured. "I wanted to put my mouth on you like Vorx is doing to me."

The frown on his face disappeared, and he swayed to his feet, walking like a drunk while tugging his pants open. His erection sprang free, and he lifted a knee to kneel on the couch beside me.

He tipped as he settled his weight on the cushion. Then kept tipping, hitting the back of the couch, and toppling over the back.

The thud of his landing shook the floor and rattled dishes somewhere. A hint of worry surfaced, but my tongue felt too big and wouldn't move the right way to say his name.

Eyes rolling, I managed to look at Vorx. His head lay between my legs, but he wasn't licking anymore.

The room swam in and out of focus again before a familiar face appeared in front of me.

"It's time to come home, Shelby," Nat said.

CHAPTER THIRTY-ONE

DISORIENTED, I TRIED TO OPEN MY EYES. THEY DIDN'T WORK THE first time but opened briefly on my second attempt. Unfortunately, nothing swam into focus before they closed again.

Something moved between my legs, not feeling good or bad. Just there. Insistent. Inside of me. But it didn't bother me as much as my inability to think straight beyond the thought that I needed to open my eyes.

"Wakey, wakey, Shelby. You don't want to miss this. Come on, girl."

A hand slapped my cheek. There wasn't any pain, but it moved my head and seemed to unglue my eyelids. My unfocused gaze twirled loosely over the ceiling.

"Come on, girl. You didn't eat as much as your grey fuck toys. Shake it off."

Whatever was moving between my legs pushed harder.

"I want you awake for this. You awake, Shelby baby? Look at me."

I managed to roll my head again and looked at Nat. He sat

beside me with his hand between my legs. His other hand went to my breast, where he pinched my nipple. Hard. It didn't hurt, though. I felt the pressure, and that was it. Just like whatever he was doing between my legs.

"There it is," he said suddenly.

He jerked his hand back then chuckled as his fingers slipped free of me. He held up a tiny white boat anchor that didn't make a lick of sense to me for a moment.

"You're not going to need this anymore," he said, setting it on my lower stomach. "The ring was too easy to remove. But you know you belong to me. So, it's time I make things more permanent. We're going to make a baby, Shelby. How would you like that?"

He traced a finger around the object on my stomach, and my brain slowly identified it—my IUD.

"But before I put a piece of myself inside of you and tie us together forever, we need to undo some of the wrongs you've done, don't we, baby?"

His hand slid over my stomach and up to my chest.

"They sure knew how to dress you. I've never seen you looking so fine. Biteable. I can't decide what I want to do first."

Scenes from the past and all the different ways he'd abused me filtered into my head. Even knowing what was coming, I was still too out of it to care.

"I'll think on it while your little dose of vitamin K wears off. You sit tight. I'll be back soon."

He patted my thigh, stood, and left the room.

I blinked at the unfamiliar door then turned my head to look around the room. It wasn't a place I knew. It wasn't home. And that bothered me. I needed to get home.

Thoughts of Turik and Vorx flitted in. Turik had fallen. Vorx too. What had Nat done to them? To us? I shook my head, trying harder to think straight.

The need to leave, to find Vorx and Turik, pushed at me. However, I couldn't sit up, no matter how hard I tried. Frustrated, I looked at the thing holding my wrist and preventing movement. Rope. Same on the other one. I lifted my head and looked down at my ankles.

A thread of fear bloomed inside me that I was tied down and spread open. The sight of my IUD resting on my stomach, right over my uterus, cleared more of my head, and what he'd said clicked into place. He'd removed my IUD and was going to rape me. Likely again and again until I was pregnant like he wanted.

A small whimper escaped me, and I tried harder to tug at my ropes. They bit into my skin, the first sensation of discomfort since I woke.

Outside the bedroom, I heard the sudden burst of male laughter. Nat wasn't alone. There were other people here. The presence of others had never stopped his abuse in the past, but I was done being quiet.

"Help me." It wasn't the yell I wanted, but a rasp. I swallowed dryly and tried clearing my throat.

"Help me." Better. Louder.

Nat walked back into the room.

"What's that, baby? Are you asking for something?"

My head was clear enough now to hear the warning in his tone and understand the promise in his angry gaze. Submit or be subjugated with fists.

"You don't own me. I'm no longer yours."

"Sweetheart, you will always be mine," he said, loosening his belt. "Looks like you just need help remembering that."

Instead of hitting me, he tossed the belt aside.

"A baby moving around inside of you will help—something for you to look after. Protect. I hear losing a baby is hard on a woman. You don't want that, do you?"

Sick understanding hit me hard like a shovel to the head, and I mentally staggered. But I didn't fall. I would never fall again for him.

"You don't own me," I said again, louder. Angrier.

"Oh, I do." He jerked his pants down just enough for his inadequate tan dick to emerge and knelt on the bed between my knees. "And I'm good to you. So good to you that I lubed you up while looking for this piece of trash." He tossed the IUD aside. "See? I want you to feel good, baby. Nothing but the best for you."

Tears slid down my cheeks as I fought the rope holding me in place.

"Raping me won't keep me here. Putting a baby in me won't keep me here. Any baby you put inside of me won't have a chance, no matter what I do. So I will sacrifice everything as many times as it takes until I escape or die trying."

His face turned red even as he smiled at me.

"Then you're going to learn a lot of hard lessons."

A loud crash came from the other room as he positioned himself at my entrance.

"And this will be the last time I do this the nice way."

The door flew open behind him. I couldn't see who it was, only the sudden appearance of two grey hands on each side of Nat's head a second before blood and gore sprayed me. The headless body between my legs started to tip forward, and I closed my eyes.

The weight disappeared. Something gently brushed over

my face, and after a few swipes, I braved opening my eyes because I had to know.

Turik's worried gaze swept over my face. He didn't ask if I was all right; he simply untied me while a single tear tracked down his cheek, matching the tears running down mine. When I was free, he eased my legs closed. I could feel how his hands were shaking and reached out to capture one in my own.

He made a pained sound when I brought his bloody digits to my lips.

"You're alive, Turik. And so am I. Vorx?" I asked, afraid of the answer.

"Alive and very angry," Vorx said from the doorway.

I looked over at him. He was just as bloody as Turik, but there weren't any tears tracking down his cheeks. The rage filling his eyes wouldn't allow for it.

"Take me home," I said simply.

Turik helped me to my feet. Vorx ripped the quilt from the bed and wrapped me in the blanket underneath it. I understood why when Turik carried me outside. We weren't in Tolerance anymore. Several fey milled around the yard, looking equally angry as they tossed bodies into a pile.

"Is that all of them?" I asked.

Turik grunted.

"Good." I lay my head against his shoulder and let him carry me the short distance back home.

The fey with us split off as soon as we cleared the wall. I saw one of them stop to talk to another fey, who looked in my direction. The remorse and anger in his expression were too much for me, and I closed my eyes to block everything out until I was ready to deal with it, a skill I'd learned long ago.

When we reached the house, Turik sat on the couch and

held me until Vorx returned, freshly washed, and took over. After Turik bathed, Vorx carried me to the shower where they washed me together. Their touch, while infinitely gentle, didn't linger anywhere. They removed all traces of blood from my face and hair, and when they finished, Vorx left me in Turik's care to fetch a towel.

I tipped my face up to look at Turik.

"I think I need some face kisses," I said, tiredly closing my eyes.

He lightly pressed his lips to my eyelids then methodically covered every inch of skin from forehead to chin. Each kiss soothed a small portion of my bruised soul. And, when he finished, I sighed, letting out some of the hurt and hate for Nat and everything he ever did or made me feel.

"I saw you fall then noticed Vorx had passed out, too. The last thing I saw before blacking out was Nat's face. Nothing made sense when I came to, but I remember him admitting to drugging us. I'm guessing it was in the food we ate. Then he reached into me and pulled out my IUD. It was the birth control I had put in when I realized I'd married a monster. He pulled it out and said he was going to put a baby in me. But he didn't get the chance. You both came."

Vorx wrapped me in a towel from behind, and I felt him set his forehead on the back of my head. His shuddering exhale warmed my shoulder.

"He's gone," I said. "He can't hurt us again. Tell me what happened. To me, it seemed like everything happened so fast. Like no more than twenty minutes had passed. But I know that wasn't the case since he'd somehow gotten me outside of Tolerance."

"We woke up, and you weren't here," Turik said. "We

looked for you, and when we knew you weren't in the house, we asked our brothers if anyone saw you. No one did, but Eitri saw men go over the wall. Men who were supposed to be helping collect supplies for the new community. Men who others saw near our house. They were carrying a large rug between the two of them as they left.

"You warned us that Nat would come for you, so we followed them. We reached the house when you told him—" He swallowed hard, and Vorx lifted his head.

"You said he would rape you, and you would never stop trying to escape, no matter the cost," Vorx finished.

I nodded slowly, understanding how much hearing that had scared them. But there wasn't anything I could say to take away the sting of the truth that I would have died trying to get away from Nat.

"Any chance we can snuggle in my bed for the next few days?" I asked instead.

CHAPTER THIRTY-TWO

FOR THE NEXT SEVERAL HOURS, WE SIMPLY LAY IN A TANGLE OF bodies, touching in subtle ways as if to reassure each other that we were really there and okay. I fell asleep with my head on Turik's chest and Vorx's arm over my waist.

The next morning, I woke to fingers in my hair and another touch trailing along my arm. I felt cocooned in a blanket of safety and comfort. The terror of the day before no longer crawled under my skin. It seemed more like a memory that belonged to another life—a life before Vorx and Turik and happiness.

While I was feeling better, I wasn't sure about my guys. Usually, they were careful not to do anything that would wake me.

"Are we better today?" I asked without opening my eyes.

There was a moment of silence, and Turik exhaled heavily.

"Not yet," Vorx said. "But soon."

"Talk to me. What's still bothering you?"

"Nat took you. Vorx and I were both there, and he still took you. We promised to keep you safe. Always," Turik said, a hint of anger in his tone. But I knew it wasn't directed at me. It was self-loathing.

Frowning, I idly traced patterns over his skin and tried to come up with something to say that would help them move past yesterday.

"Nothing that happened is either of your faults."

"You warned us," Vorx said.

"I did. But not so you would feel guilty when something happened. If I hadn't warned you, would you have known to look for me when I disappeared, or would you have maybe thought I'd left on my own? After all, that's your biggest fear, isn't it? And sometimes, our biggest fears have a way of changing the way we would normally think."

They both grunted.

"Nothing that happened is your fault," I repeated. "And I'm glad you came for me. This time and the first time.

"Thank you for feeding me, protecting me, and holding me while I sleep. For giving me little kisses when I'm sad and watching me smile when I'm happy. It turns out I wanted all of that as much as you did. As much as you both did."

I leveraged myself up so I could kiss Turik. A real one that conveyed everything I felt for him.

Easing away, I looked him in the eyes.

"I love you, Turik. Today. Tomorrow. And every day of my life. Forever."

He closed his eyes and hugged me tight, momentarily pulling me from Vorx's hold.

When Turik released me, I turned to Vorx and gently cupped his cheeks.

"I would have never thought it possible to feel this way for two people. But I love you too, Vorx. Just as much. It burns fiercely inside of me. So much that I take back what I told you. There is no other woman out there waiting for you. She's right here in front of you, and she will do anything to bring you as much joy as you bring her."

He moved fast, claiming my lips in a kiss that left me panting and breathless. I kissed his chin and ran my hand down his abs. However, he caught my wrist before I could reach the band of his athletic shorts. He brought my hand to his mouth and kissed my fingers.

"You should rest some more."

I smiled at his consideration.

"I'm fine."

"You have new bruises," Turik said.

"I'm sure I do. But that's just part of life. We need to work together to move past what happened yesterday. I want you to keep touching me and reminding me what a gentle, loving man feels like. I want to erase the memory of his touch once and for all. Now, what do you need from me? How can I help you?"

Vorx groaned and buried his face in the curve of my neck, kissing my skin tenderly.

"We need you to stay close to us. We need to see you," Turik said. "We need to know you're safe."

"Okay. Done. I won't go anywhere without you. Except for the bathroom. That's still not going to be a team sport. But I'll talk to you through the door if that helps."

Turik grunted and kissed my temple.

"Now, is it still Vorx's turn, or does passing out between my legs count as a finish for him?" I asked with some sass.

Vorx nipped my neck in reply. I shivered and grinned like a fool. Lifting his head, he smirked at me then rolled away to tug off his shorts.

"You'll tell me if anything hurts."

"I will," I promised.

He lifted me so I lay on top of him, continuing his leisurely exploration of my neck and jawline. At some point, I changed position to straddle his waist and shed my shirt.

His gaze immediately went to my breasts, and he frowned. New bruises marked the area around my nipples.

"Make me forget," I said softly. "Make us all forget."

He sat up, and his lips gently grazed over them. An ache that had nothing to do with the markings slowly grew, and my nipples pebbled. He took them into his mouth, tenderly sucking and licking until I was panting with need.

"I want you inside of me. Please."

"Not like this," Vorx said.

"How?" I asked, pushing myself off his chest.

He lifted me and sat up, setting me next to the bed.

"Undress," he said.

It was my turn to smirk as I hooked my fingers in my underwear and turned, already bending to slide them down my ass. The sight of Turik brought me up short. He sat in the watcher chair, his gaze hungrily sweeping over me like it always did when I was with Vorx. Hungry and concerned.

Although I knew they trusted each other, they supervised each other as if they didn't. That needed to end. We needed complete trust.

I leaned forward and brushed my lips against his. I could see the surprise in his eyes before he opened his mouth and kissed me with enough passion that the world and all its troubles melted away.

This, I thought. *This is what we need.*

His hands gently smoothed over my well-kissed breasts before slowly pulling away and waving me back toward Vorx.

"Continue," Turik said with a wink.

Smiling, I glanced over my shoulder at Vorx, who was sitting on the edge of the bed. His gaze tracked every move as I slowly slid the last bit of material covering me down my legs. When my fingers reached my ankles, and I was about to step out of them, I felt a hand on my lower back.

"I love when you do this," he said, a hand running over my hip.

"How much?" I asked.

"This much," he said a moment before I felt his tongue teasing my folds.

I groaned and reached out to brace myself on Turik's knees and widen my stance. Vorx took every inch I gave. His tongue slid over me again and again, making my clit throb with need and my core ache for more.

"More," I panted.

Vorx stood and fitted his swollen head at my entrance.

"Look at me," Turik said.

I blinked and focused on Turik's face as Vorx carefully worked his way inside of me. I could see the worry there again.

"Kiss me," I whispered.

Turik leaned forward and kissed me, his lips gently exploring mine. This was the first time he'd interacted with me while Vorx and I were having sex. I would have thought it would be too much, but it wasn't. It was just right. I needed this. Them. To feel together.

Vorx finally seated himself fully with a groan.

"Is it too much?" he asked.

Turik stopped kissing me, giving me a chance to evaluate.

Vorx was big, filling me to the point of aching. But it was exactly what I needed. I couldn't feel the shadow of Nat's touch anymore. Only Vorx. Everywhere.

"No. It's perfect."

He started moving gingerly, the friction building that tension inside of me. My nipples ached, and I brought one of Turik's hands to them.

His fingers gently rolled and plucked the peaks.

"Not like this," Turik said suddenly. "Like yesterday. On the edge of the bed."

Vorx's arms wrapped around my waist. He lifted me without withdrawing and backed up a step. The position changed the angle and added pressure to just the right spot, and I rotated my hips in appreciation. Vorx growled and gave a small thrust in response.

"Feet up, our Shelby," Turik said, guiding my shins to the mattress.

Vorx sat, pulling me with him, so I rode him backward. I glanced over my shoulder and saw him laying back on the bed as he ran a hand down my side and gripped my hips. His thumbs circled over my ass cheeks and lifted me to reseat me on his length. I leaned forward a little, changing the angle, and lifted myself again. His pupils dilated as I sank back down, and I echoed the sentiment.

Lips parted, I slowly rode him, hands braced on his thighs, loving the feel of him filling me.

"This is a good view," Vorx said, his breathing growing harsh.

"A very good view," Turik agreed a moment before his mouth closed over my nipple.

I gasped and looked down at him where he knelt between

our legs. Vorx's hand on my hips took over, maintaining a steady slow rhythm while Turik's mouth explored me. The dual sensations fried my brain. Threading my fingers through Turik's hair, I held on as that tension inside of me coiled tighter.

The touch of Turik's hands on my knees barely registered until he nudged them wider. He tore his mouth from my breast and said something I didn't catch. I was so close. Just a little more, and I'd go over.

"Shelby," he said, gently tipping my chin so I'd look him in the eyes. "Lean back, my love. My life."

Smiling at him, I leaned back, bracing my arms on the mattress.

Both he and Vorx groaned.

"I need to taste you," Turik said.

My core clenched hard around Vorx at the thought of Turik tasting me now, like this, while Vorx was right there, still arching in and out of me.

Vorx hissed out a breath. "She liked that idea." He picked up speed. "Taste her."

Turik leaned in. His tongue pressed against my clit as Vorx went deep. That was all I needed to fall over the edge. The first wave of my orgasm made lights flicker in my peripheral. The second and third forced a low moan from my lips.

After that, the only detail I grasped was pleasure. So much of it as Turik licked me, and Vorx thrust inside of me. Eventually, Turik stopped licking and plucked me off Vorx to carry me to the shower.

My core hadn't yet stopped twitching when Vorx joined us.

"Do you need more time, our Shelby?" Vorx asked.

I looked up into Turik's hungry gaze and slowly shook my head. He grinned and passed me to Vorx.

"The wall is still too cold," he said, lightly kissing my lips before having his way with me.

Twenty minutes later, we were clean and out of hot water. They worked together to dry me, Turik taking care of my front while Vorx meticulously addressed my backside. I grinned at the pair, loving every second of the attention they gave me.

I never wanted this to end, and now, the fear that it would was gone forever.

Finally, I could live.

"What do you say to some non-drugged breakfast and some feight club? I think I see a helluva lot more time with Hannah in my future because I am never again going to find myself the victim of someone's abuse."

"Except maybe Hannah's," Vorx said, making Turik chuckle.

It was a good sound. A healing one. And with it, I knew we would be okay.

EPILOGUE

"I'M SURE EVERYTHING IS FINE," I SAID YET AGAIN. "I'M PROBABLY dehydrated or something. We've been going at it non-stop. Maybe I just need a longer recovery time."

I honestly hoped that wasn't the case, though. I loved back-to-back sessions. The feel of them filling me again when I was still sensitive was my new addiction. Or sessions where the other one pitched in to make it even more mind-blowing. A slow screw and oral at the same time? My core clenched at the thought of it.

And I couldn't quite hide the wince.

Damn wince was what got me in trouble into the first place. Turik had been entering me oh-so-slowly from behind, my morning wake up call, and Vorx had been watching from the chair. The moment Turik reached my cervix, I'd winced at an uncomfortable ache. Vorx had caught my reaction—of course he had—and it hadn't just been game over for fun time after that. No, it had resulted in complete "the sky is falling" panic, but with "we broke her pussy" fear.

I huffed out a sigh and glanced at the houses around us.

"Seriously, you two. This is completely unnecessary and far too early to go knocking on someone's door."

Neither acknowledged that I was even speaking. I rolled my eyes and settled in for an embarrassing visit with Cassie.

Vorx jogged ahead and knocked on the door. Turik exhaled shakily.

"It's not broken," I said for the hundredth time. Eden was going to laugh her ass off when she heard this one. Hell, the whole feight club gang would.

The door to Cassie's home was opened by a rather stern looking Kerr, who glanced at me and Turik as he carried me up the walk then to Vorx. Vorx said something quietly, and a slight frown crossed Kerr's face before he opened the door wider and motioned us to enter.

"Cassie is sleeping," he said when he shut the door behind us. "I'll go wake her."

"Please don't," I begged. "I'm fine. Truly."

Kerr's gaze flicked over me, wrapped in a blanket in Turik's arms, then to Turik and Vorx.

"You can take her to the office," he said before walking away.

I made a distinctly annoyed face at being ignored—again—and silently stewed as Turik carried me down the hall to the makeshift exam room.

"Don't worry, Shelby," Turik said, finally letting go of me. "Cassie will know how to fix you."

"I love you Turik, but right now, I'm not having very loving thoughts for either of you. It was just a wince."

"We've both watched you. We know what it looks like when we go too deep or thrust too hard. This was a new look. This was pain."

"It wasn't pain, it was discomfort and probably due to a little overuse yesterday. Wasn't eight times the magic number that had Eden sitting on ice? But no, you couldn't just think, 'Hey, maybe we need to cut back,' like a normal person would, or offer me some damn ice. No, you rolled me up like a cigar and carted me off to the doctor before dawn. For a wince!" I ended in an agitated whisper.

The first hint of doubt finally crept into Turik's expression.

"Listen, I know that what happened last week scared you both. It scared me too. But a very smart person told me that we can't live our lives in fear. That it holds us back from seeing the potential of our futures. You need to ease up. Like maybe no more standing outside the bathroom door. I thought I'd be okay with it, but I'm not ten percent of the time."

"Good morning," a sleep-tousled red head said tiredly as she entered the room. "What seems to be the problem?"

"Nothing," I said quickly. "We're truly sorry for waking you up."

Her gaze flicked to my guys, who were sharing another long look.

"I think we hurt Shelby," Turik said finally, and I dropped my head in my hands. Flames of embarrassment licked at my face.

"Okay. Out. Both of you. The kids are going to wake up soon, and Kerr could use the help."

They left quickly, and she closed the door behind them. Facing me, she smiled kindly and took in my wrapped appearance.

"Naked?" she asked.

"Yep. They didn't let me get dressed first. I'm not even sure they heard me."

"Likely, they can hear you just fine now. Those ears are wickedly keen. Why don't you tell me what has them so worried?"

The flush in my face intensified but I ignored it.

"I winced during intercourse. It wasn't painful. Just a little sore."

"Totally understandable," she said with an easy nod. "How many times a day are you...?"

"Eight yesterday. The wince was during the first time this morning."

"I see. Did you do anything new yesterday? New angle? Position?"

"Nope. And they're always very careful."

"They? Are you having intercourse with both at the same time?"

A choked sound escaped me.

"Hell no. Both of them are super-sized. I'm stretched with one hole stuffed. No thank you on two. It's one at a time for this girl."

Cassie held up her hands. "Even if it weren't, I'm not judging. Just troubleshooting. Frankly, I'm not a gynecologist. There's not a whole lot I know about the topic outside my own experiences and what others have shared." She stood and rummaged through the cabinets and took out a box. "Which means I'd like you to consider taking this."

She handed me a pregnancy test, and I felt my stomach drop.

"Seriously?" I asked quietly, my stunned thoughts churning.

It couldn't be possible. Nat had removed my IUD eight days ago. Or was it ten now? Either way, it was definitely less than two weeks. I shouldn't have had time to ovulate yet, should I?

"I take it this isn't something you've considered?" Cassie asked in a gentle voice.

"Not really. I mean, yeah. In the back of my head. But I've just been taking one day at a time and not really thinking, you know?"

"I do know. That's what most of us are doing. Taking one day at a time. There's nothing wrong with that." She motioned for me to follow her across the hall and left me alone in the bathroom.

I took the test, paced the bathroom for the appropriate amount of time, then stared at the results in disbelief. The indication was there. Faint, but there. Pregnant.

A range of emotions rushed through me. Joy. Worry. Wonder. Hesitation. Fear. I wasn't sure exactly what to feel. I'd wanted kids before marrying Nat. But would that baby be any safer now? I knew Turik and Vorx wanted babies, but they were also nervous about having them.

Shit.

They were already freaked out about my health and safety. What would they be like after this?

A knock on the door interrupted my growing apprehension.

"Are you ready for some company?" Cassie asked.

I opened the door and held up the test.

"Well, we have an answer for the tenderness then, don't we," she said kindly. "Would you like to talk privately with me or—"

Turik and Vorx appeared around the corner.

"You know what's wrong with her?" Turik asked.

Cassie watched me, letting me decide how I wanted to handle this.

"There's nothing wrong with me," I said. "I'm pregnant."

Both of my guys paled but didn't stop coming at me. I was up in Vorx's arms and hugged between the two of them.

"Don't worry, Shelby. You're safe. The baby is safe. We will ask our brothers if there is another who wants to live with us."

"No," I said quickly. "You two are plenty. I know I'm safe. I know you two can handle this. We'll be fine."

"The tenderness should fade," Cassie said. "You should be perfectly fine to resume normal activities. Let Shelby be the judge of what's okay for her."

I shot Cassie a grateful smile.

"There are some prenatal vitamins I'd like to send with you. The fey are looking for more in the hopes that pregnancies will increase."

She passed the bottle to Turik.

"If you have any questions or concerns, I'm here. Julie and Nancy are also good resources if I'm not available. We're pooling our knowledge on this."

"Thank you, Cassie," Turik said.

They hustled me out of that house so quickly I wasn't sure what was going on until we arrived at our own and they stripped me of my blanket to take turns listening to my stomach.

"We will need more food," Vorx said.

"Snack cakes," Turik agreed. "That makes Angel's baby move."

Vorx's hand slid over the curve of my hips, and I knew what he was thinking.

"Maybe some healthier food options, okay? Like vegetables and lean meats and fruit. There's more nutrition in those for the baby."

Vorx grunted, and I knew I was still going to get some fattening snack cakes.

Turik's hands ran up my body to gently knead my breasts.

"The other females had sore breasts when they were first pregnant. This is supposed to help."

They didn't hurt, but his touch sure did feel good. My nipples pebbled, and he noticed.

"I think it's still Vorx's turn, isn't it?" I asked.

Vorx growled, and his teeth skimmed my shoulder.

I closed my eyes and welcomed him home.

AUTHOR'S NOTE

Shelby's story was only supposed to be a novella. She was supposed to fall for Turik and have a happily ever after. I told her what to do, but she was so starved for love and affection (the real kind) and so afraid to feel safe again that there was only one answer. Two fey!

Turik and Vorx saw Shelby for the miracle she was. A female willing to love both of them because they wanted to work together to keep a female and any children she might have safe. Better survival rate in a world where the infected are getting smarter and smarter, right? I know so many readers are tired of reverse harems, but I hope this one didn't put you off. This will be the only one in the series. However, if there is enough reader demand, I am open to writing more of these kinds of relationships in a new world.

I learned so much writing Shelby's book. The biggest bit of information was that my sister-in-law (8 years my younger) is scary smart about things I didn't even know about. You can thank her for that vitamin K scene. Now, I'm smarter about date rape drugs too. (I'm not sure if that's a good or bad thing, but holy crap, date rape drugs are not okay!)

I also learned a whole bunch about IUDs. Like you can get pregnant right away after an IUD removal due to sperm already inside of you (since those buggers can live for DAYS). While I knew about swimmer longevity, it was still an eye opener for me to realize you could get pregnant from intercourse prior to the removal.

While this story was supposed to be a cute little novella in the Rez world, something light and fluffy for me to work on while I was dealing with some post-COVID and post-surgery brain fog, I don't regret that something obviously went way wrong (or right, depending on how you look at it). It was fun to explore a relationship this complex and get a glimpse of what non-fey people are doing and thinking.

I truly hope you enjoyed this extra addition to the Resurrection world. Now that this is out of the way, it's time to focus on Molev and the finale.

Make sure to stay up to date on all my projects by signing up for my newsletter at mjhaag.melissahaag.com/subscribe.

Until next time, happy reading!

Melissa

THE
RESURRECTION CHRONICLES

Humor, romance, and sexy dark fey!

BOOK 1: DEMON EMBER

In a world going to hell, Mya must learn to accept help from her new-found demon protector in order to find her family as a zombie-like plague spreads.

BOOK 2: DEMON FLAMES

As hellhounds continue to roam and the zombie plague spreads, Drav leads Mya to the source of her troubles—Ernisi, an underground Atlantis and Drav's home. There Mya learns that the shadowy demons, who've helped devastate her world, are not what they seem.

BOOK 3: DEMON ASH

While in Ernisi, cites were been bombed and burned in an attempt to stop the plague. Now, Marauders, hellhounds, and the infected are doing their best to destroy what's left of the world. It's up to Mya and Drav to save it.

BOOK 4: DEMON ESCAPE

While running from zombies, hellhounds, and the people who kept her prisoner, Eden encounters a new creature. He claims he only wants to protect her. Eden must decide who the real devils are between man and demon, and choosing wrong could cost her life.

BOOK 5: DEMON DECEPTION

Grieving from the loss of her husband and youngest child, Cassie lives in fear of losing her remaining daughter. To gain protection, Cassie knows she needs to sleep with one of the dark fey and give him the one thing she isn't sure she can. Her heart.

THE
RESURRECTION
CHRONICLES

The apocalyptic adventure continues!

BOOK 6: DEMON NIGHT

Angel's growing weaker by the day and needs help. In exchange for food, she agrees to give Shax advice regarding how to win over Hannah. If Angel can help make that happen, just maybe she won't be kicked out when her fellow survivors find out she's pregnant.

BOOK 7: DEMON DAWN

In a post-apocalyptic world, Benna is faced with the choice of trading her body and heart to the dark fey in order to survive the infected.

BOOK 8: DEMON DISGRACE

Hannah is drinking away her life to stanch the bleeding pain from past trauma. Merdon, a dark fey with a violent history, relentlessly sets out to show her there's something worth living for.

BOOK 9: DEMON FALL

June never planned to fall in love. She had her eyes on the prize: a career and independence. Too bad the world ended and stole those options from her. Maybe falling in love had been the better choice after all.

Beauty and the Beast with seductively dark twists!

BOOK 1: DEPRAVITY

When impoverished, beautiful Benella is locked inside the dark and magical estate of the beast, she must bargain for her freedom if she wants to see her family again.

BOOK 2: DECEIT

Safely hidden within the estate's enchanted walls, Benella no longer has time to fear her tormentors. She's too preoccupied trying to determine what makes the beast so beastly. In order to gain her freedom, she must find a way to break the curse, but first, she must help him become a better man while protecting her heart.

BOOK 3: DEVASTATION

Abused and rejected, Benella strives to regain a purpose for her life, and finds herself returning to the last place she ever wanted to see. She must learn when it is right to forgive and when it is time to move on.

TALES OF CINDER

Be careful what you wish for...

PREQUEL: DISOWNED

In a world where the measure of a person rarely goes beneath the surface, Margaret Thoning refuses to play by its rules. She walks away from everything she's ever known to risk her heart and her life for the people who matter most.

BOOK 1: DEFIANT

When the sudden death of Eloise's mother points to forbidden magic, Eloise's life quickly goes from fairy tale to nightmare. Kaven, the prince's manservant, is Eloise's prime suspect. However, when dark magic is used, nothing is as simple as it seems.

BOOK 2: DISDAIN

Cursed to silence, Eloise is locked in the tattered remains of her once charming life. The smoldering spark of her anger burns for answers and revenge. However, games of magic can have dire consequences.

BOOK 3: DAMNATION

With the reason behind her mother's death revealed, Eloise must prevent her stepsisters from marrying the prince and exact her revenge. However, a secret of the royal court strikes a blow to her plans. Betrayed, Eloise will question how far she's willing to go for revenge.